D0889617

Cream Puff Murder

A Seagrass Sweets Cozy Mystery

Sandi Scott

GRATICE
PRESS

Table of Contents

CHAPTER 1

"GO FORTH, WEE delectable ones, and bring joy unto the influential women of the world."

Ashley Adams beamed as she placed the final strawberry garnish on her crème brûlée fleet. Stepping back to admire her work of culinary art, she was momentarily distracted by the waiters, silently carrying platters of her chocolate éclairs, coconut macaroons and other sweets out into the banquet hall.

While she gazed at her masterpiece, her thoughts turned to her recent bout of luck in securing the catering contract for Seagrass's annual Women of Influence awards banquet.

Even though she had her old friend Ryan to thank for the introduction, she knew that it was her and Patty's collective expertise in French cuisine that had cinched the deal. Growing up in Seagrass, she never dreamed of even entering the elegant Gulf Coast Women's Club, let alone catering a major event there.

As her thoughts wandered over how her new life back in Seagrass had been coming together more easily than anticipated, she noticed her show-stopping croquembouche, a cone tower of heavenly cream puffs adorned with divine, edible flowers and perfectly spun caramel, carried precariously by the waiter, making Ashley wince in barely-restrained horror. Crossing her fingers, she hoped he had better balance than she did as she did her best not to follow and fuss at him, while Patty stood at the other kitchen door window, shaking her head disapprovingly.

"Who knew we'd find more gourmands at the Women of Influence banquet than that high school football awards ceremony?" Patty checked the state of her tight bun in a mirror, even though her pale blonde locks wouldn't dare allow a strand to spring out of place. "Why spend all this time making the best crab cakes and beef wellington they could ever taste if it goes straight from fork to gullet?"

Ashley smiled at Patty's disgruntled face. A Francophile in her mid-fifties, Patty had brought more than her world-renowned talent as chef when she left Paris to come to Seagrass; her French manners hung on her like an expensive fur coat.

"They're career women, Patty, like you," said Ashley. "Probably just starving from all that hard work."

Patty's scowl broke out into a small smile. Just like Ashley's decadent chocolate truffles, she was all soft, sweet, and gooey inside, once you got past her hard, outer shell.

"Hard work?" Patty scoffed. "They've been sipping cocktails on beach chairs all day. Well, aOfter all that lounging and gourmanding, maybe the exhaustion will slow them down for dessert. Your pastries are too delicious not to relish."

Ashley tried to suppress the rush of pleasure she felt at Patty's compliment. She knew if she blushed, Patti would only scold her and warn her not to let it go to her head.

Though they were far from the French kitchen of L'Oiseau Bleu where they met, they were both very proud and enthusiastic about offering fine dining to the community of Seagrass, Texas. Patty, owner of the French cuisine catering company The Southern Bird, and Ashley, with her French dessert catering company Seagrass Sweets, were the perfect partners and did most of their jobs together.

"Glad you left your quaint flat in the 13th arrondissement to return home?" Patty asked with a comical fluttering of her lashes. They both knew that by "quaint flat" Patty meant small, expensive dump of an apartment.

"Of course. I'm finally building my dream in a place I love instead of trying to love a place I never quite fit. How about you? Was taking a risk on an intern pâtissière and opening a catering business worth leaving Paris behind?"

Patty shrugged playfully and smiled. "We'll see."

"Oh, come on. French cuisine catering here in Seagrass—where BBQ reigns supreme. You've already received rave reviews in the local fine dining magazines. You're my hero."

"Really? How about you? Your own French dessert catering business—so soon. Look at us now — we're hot in the culinary community. Two women in charge of their own companies."

Ashley giggled, dizzy with the whole scenario. "You're giving me chills, Patty."

They both laughed as they continued with last minute preparations and details.

The sound of a woman's voice could be heard through the swinging doors. Up on the stage, the president of the Gulf Coast Housing

Association, Hope McCay, was speaking at the podium. A childhood friend of Ashley's, she was still a self-described "redhead unafraid to wear red lipstick." She was talking about the preservation of the Gulf Coast and Seagrass, interspersed with applause and occasional cheers of encouragement from the audience.

"Seagrass has managed to support tourism without losing the charm and serenity of a small Gulf Coast fishing town. That's no easy feat, especially since we do so while preserving our wonderful environment and natural resources." More applause came from the audience.

Ashley grinned and nodded as she taste-tested her ginger-laced glacé cherries. "Amen, sister."

"While the larger port cities cater to spring-breakers and industrial interests, weekend warriors flock to Seagrass's historic, beachside inns and quaint villas on the Colorado River. We have to ensure that any business entities seeking a foothold in our beautiful city do not destroy the area's delicate ecosystems."

A male voice called out, "Bravo!" Many bouts of laughter and copycats repeating his exclamation rang out in the banquet hall.

Patty responded with an excite burst of clapping. "Might I add, with that surge of up-scale clientele here in Seagrass—in a culinary scene dominated by fast food franchises—we are very lucky to have tapped into the market of fine dining and catering, the delicate ecosystems notwithstanding?"

She squinted through the window. "Oh, they've got the dessert table arrangement all wrong, even after I drew them a labeled diagram. These mess-hall waiters will be the death of me!"

Parisian waiters would generally undergo years of training in fine dining service, so all waiters were especially subject to Patty's scrutiny. A twinkle cracked the icy surface of her blue eyes. "Why don't you go and make it right, before the speech is over?"

Ashley peered nervously into the dimly lit dining room. A man was standing in the hallway near the dessert table, rather than sitting around the dining tables like everyone else. Ashley recognized the outline of his messy, brown curls. She turned to busy herself with cleaning up. "Maybe you should go and make sure it's done right."

Patty grabbed her arm with the speed and ruthlessness of a snake sinking fangs into its prey. "Oh, no, you don't. I caught you sneaking peeks at him during cocktail hour. Now you have to go, and then tell me all about him. That's how it works."

She pointed at Ashley with the authority that only French-trained head chefs could master, almost poking out the eye of a straggling waiter.

"Patty, I've already told you about Ryan."

"Not the important stuff. All I know is that you worked a dead-end IT job together before you came to Paris. Those are the facts—I want the feels."

Ashley smiled as she remembered.

"You know, we had a lot of fun in that basement office. We called ourselves the 'Below-Grounders against the Above-Grounders.' Most of the people we helped couldn't figure out the most basic of tasks, like the relationship between their computer's power cord and the need to actually plug it into the outlet, and Ryan and I kept each other sane. But he had a girlfriend and I was with Serge at the time, so there were no feels, Patty."

"Sounds so romantic." Patty scoffed, stirring her au jus.

"Romance is relative, snooty-pants." Ashley retorted as she made her way to the door.

Patty laughed. "Anyway, what's he doing here? Unless he just can't stand to be away from you."

"The news station sponsoring the banquet is one of his clients. He has his own web design and IT business now, so it has nothing to do with me, if you must know." She tried brushing off the layer of flour that clung to her chef jacket. "He was a good friend, and when I left for Paris, it was—abrupt. I never got to say a proper goodbye."

Patty raised an eyebrow. "You two seem to have put that past you, seeing as he basically got both of us this 'magnifique' banquet tonight."

Ashley chuckled. "Forgive and forget, I suppose." She didn't need to see Patty's face to know what look she was giving her. "Okay. You're right. I suppose I shouldn't leave without thanking him for getting us this gig."

"Wait." Patty held up her finger as she looked critically at Ashley's uniform.

"Are you kidding me?" Ashley held out her arms for examination, knowing that resistance was futile. "This is a quarantined uniform. You've already inspected it."

"Dog hair is the most cunning and persistent contagion of all, hiding until it's safe to disperse and multiply." Patty's nostrils flared as she leaned closer.

Ashley sighed, thinking it might have been easier to keep her dog Dizzy plastic-wrapped at all times.

"I get that this is a most upscale—Hey! Whoa! Are you sniffing me? Have you no shame?"

"I'm a chef. I can sniff out a single dog hair better than a dog can—and that single hair can ruin a whole dish—but never mind, you're clear." She smoothed Ashley's uniform with her hands, then tapped her on the shoulders, signaling the all-clear.

Laughing, Ashley pushed the door open and made her way to the tables to rearrange her desserts.

"Ma'am, are you lost?" a voice whispered from the hallway. Even though she couldn't see him, she heard Ryan's smile in his voice.

While some people possessed "resting grumpy faces," Ashley had the curse of the "resting lost face." Even after she had been working at her old job for years, the Above-Grounders had continued to ask if she needed help finding the cafeteria.

"Hmm, well, I think I can find my way back to the kitchen, but luckily, there's this weirdo lurking in the darkness to help me if I can't find my way," Ashley whispered back as she joined him, leaning casually against the mahogany-paneled wood.

Ryan sniggered. "I ducked out to the bath-room when they served the entrees. I made the mistake of telling my table I worked in IT, and then they all wanted my help uploading pictures of their food."

Ashley laughed. "Must have been out-of-towners. I haven't even had one local put me on tech-support speed dial after telling them I used to work with computers. I think most of them are too stubborn to ask for help."

He leaned into the light enough for Ashley to reacquaint herself with his blue eyes.

"Yeah, they were Houstoners. Three CEOs, a neurosurgeon and a law firm partner at my table, and yet picking a photo filter is apparently too high-stakes of a call to make themselves." He motioned toward a far table. "There is one local here who's guilty of calling me for free tech-support. My college buddy—he owns a construction company here—Eddie Vay. I think you know him, actually."

"Oh, yeah," Ashley replied, faking a smile rather than saying more.

She'd never cared for Eddie, who had cut off one of her pigtails when she was in second grade. As an adult, he'd run most of the area's smaller construction companies, like her father's, out of business, undercutting them on price in ways that no one could understand. Ashley hadn't talked to Eddie in years; now that she was back in Seagrass, she was in no hurry to do so.

She heard the back door down the hall close softly. A petite woman peeked around the corner.

"Is she almost done?"

It was Colleen Abramson, the secretary of Bobby McCay who was not only the father of Hope, the speaker, but also one of the largest real estate holders in the county. Known for her cheery disposition and tight spiral curls, Colleen was now almost unrecognizable with a messy ponytail and agitation crowding her face.

They all stared at the podium where Hope, with her knack for public speaking, was gracefully enunciating every syllable without losing her smile.

"But as we move forward, Seagrass can stand with pride, embracing the future without losing the past. That's why I will make sure that any developers who do business here in Seagrass adhere to the same values that we, the people of Seagrass, have and hold dear. I have a four-part plan I'd like to share with you."

Ashley finally answered Colleen's question. "Sounds like she still has most of the speech left. Is everything okay?"

"Oh." Startled, Colleen shook her head as if she'd forgotten where they were. "No, yeah, it's fine." She turned to leave but then stopped, seeming to be deep in thought. Turning back, she smiled apologetically at Ashley.

"Say, would it be too much to ask for the desserts to be served straight after Hope's done up there? I only ask as Bobby is getting a little tired. Even though he loves his little girl and he wanted to stay for her speech, I can tell that he's ready to turn in. Is that okay?"

"Sure. We're all ready to rock and roll, honey."

Colleen smiled. "Thanks." Then she dashed off in a hurry to wait by the bathroom door, reading and typing on her phone with agitation.

"Looks like someone needs a cream puff." Ryan quipped.

Ashley grabbed the sleeve of a passing

waiter.

"Let's get the desserts delivered to the McKay table first—straight after the speech, okay? Then you can go on with the rest."

He nodded and darted off to the kitchen without a word.

Ashley shifted her feet, causing her "no-slip" kitchen shoes to grip the wooden floor in a way that somehow tangled her legs, making her fall all over herself. Ryan chuckled and helped her up. For an IT guy, his hands were surprisingly rough with calluses on his palms from weight-lifting.

"Still tripping over nothing, I see," Ryan teased.

Feeling the blush start, she acted like there was something she had to do in the kitchen and headed straight to the bathroom. A lifetime of tripping over herself in public had taught her that the privacy of a stall was the best place to recover from the embarrassment.

Way to be smooth, Ash, she thought as she

checked herself in the mirror first, glad that her crimson cheeks were the worst of it. Despite spending the last few hours rushing around a hot kitchen, she'd managed to look somewhat presentable for her venture out into the "guest" side of the banquet. She'd pulled her chocolate-brown bob into a ponytail for work, and by the end of the night it was always exactly where she'd left it. She used to hate having hair too stubbornly straight to hold a curl, but its willfulness came in handy in her line of work.

She had only been in the stall a minute before the bathroom door was wrenched open, and she heard hushed, panicked voices. Once the door closed, the yelling started.

"You have to delete it! Forget you ever saw it. That email has nothing to do with you and me!" a man's voice said.

"I beg to differ," a female voice replied between sniffles. Through the crack, Ashley recognized the woman as Colleen, but she couldn't see the man.

21

"It has a lot to do with us and our future here in Seagrass. Plus, he's my boss—when it gets out, people will be shocked. What if they think I..."

Ashley sat, frozen to the seat. She wondered how long her legs, which she had lifted to keep her feet above the gap between the floor and the stall door, could stand it.

"Well, you don't have to be the one to tell."

"I'm not asking, Colleen; I'm warning you. This email is none of your business, and you'd best leave it alone."

Ashley heard his fast footsteps and then the heavy bathroom door closing. She peeked back through the crack to see Colleen folded over the counter, crying angrily into her hands. Ashley was torn between comforting her and not wanting her to feel embarrassed that she'd been overheard, but her legs were shaking and she couldn't hold them up much longer. Just as she resolved to come out of the stall, Colleen washed her face quickly and left the bathroom.

Someone really does need a cream puff, Ashley thought. She looked in the bathroom mirror while shaking the lactic acid out of her leg muscles. Who was Colleen talking to and what on earth could be in that email? Ashley knew Colleen's boss was Bobby McCay, but she couldn't even begin to guess what kind of secret he had that could be so shocking, nor could Ashley figure out who the man trying to protect Bobby was. It was a mystery, but Ashley saw no reason to poke her nose where it didn't belong. When she made her way out of the bathroom and down the hallway nearly colliding with Colleen, who was still staring at her phone and pacing, Ashley bit her tongue, smiled and pretended that she hadn't heard a thing.

"Oh, I'm sorry! I'm so busy, I don't know if I'm coming or going." Colleen didn't seem to suspect Ashley had overheard the argument. "I talked with the waiters," she continued. "They're ready to serve the desserts right after Hope is done."

"That's great," Colleen said with a weak smile. "Thank you."

Ashley smiled back. "Well, I hope everyone liked our food."

Colleen nodded but kept glancing at her phone. "Of course they did. You're a great chef."

"Are you okay?" Ashley dared to ask.

"Sure. Why?"

"Oh, nothing. You just seem upset or something."

The women locked eyes with each other for a moment before Colleen revealed a more convincing grin.

"Don't worry about me, sweetie. It's just been a long day, and Bobby can be very demanding. Actually—speaking of Bobby—I must go."

Ashley watched Colleen take off, only to stop and linger by the banquet hall door. Moments later, the lights brightened, signaling the end of the speech. Heads immediately turned to the dessert table, like sharks smelling blood. A crowd formed around the croquembouche, some taking pictures of Ashley's masterpiece.

She didn't mind the food photography phenomenon. Patty always said that cuisine's fleeting nature was what made it such a beautiful art; after painstakingly placing carnation petals and clover blossoms between the spun caramel, Ashley liked knowing that her work would be immortalized before disappearing down those rich gullets forever.

CHAPTER 2

THE NEXT DAY, Ashley pulled in to the back entrance of the Gulf Coast Women's Club, mentally replaying the highlights of their biggest catering job yet. Her only regret was that she had not seen Ryan again after she tripped over herself and hid in the bathroom; she found herself wishing she could have told him about some of the hilarious kitchen bloopers of the night. The dessert spread had been such a hit that she'd been too distracted with all the compliments to clean up properly, accidentally leaving behind a few baking trays.

She made her way into the kitchen and grabbed the trays. The kitchen door swung open, startling her. All the pans fell out of her grasp and clattered on the floor.

"Ashley? What're you doing here?"

It was Sheriff Mueller, staring at her with a look of apprehension. Seagrass had always been such a peaceful town, so the odd time something did happen, it could be seen on Old Man Mueller's face. Also, the fact that he wasn't at the diner drinking coffee and brushing breakfast crumbs from his grey stubble, like every other morning, meant that something really bad had happened.

"I'm getting my pans. What's wrong?"

His eyebrows scrunched together, wrinkling his forehead even more.

"You were here for the event last night, and you cooked the food?"

She nodded. "The desserts."

"Why don't you come out here with me?"

His tone was serious, but Ashley had always found a southern drawl comforting. She felt that if you had to get bad news, at least it sounded better blanketed with an accent.

A crowd of Seagrass's small police force was gathered in front of the side hallway, which was blocked off with caution tape.

"We're waitin' for the state police to get here for forensics," Mueller offered, taking a notebook from his pocket. "Would you mind answering a few questions?"

"Uh, what's this about?" She crossed her arms, wishing that she hadn't thrown on sweatpants and a Texans jersey.

He sighed, putting a hand on her shoulder.

"Colleen Abramson fell ill at the dinner last night. Someone found her in the bathroom this morning—deceased."

Her mind raced with questions. "Colleen? Dead? I just saw her. Talked with her. I stood right in front of her. How could she suddenly be dead?"

"We don't know much yet. Bobby says she grew ill near the end of the night and left to go to the bathroom. There was a miscommunication, and everyone at her table assumed that someone else had seen her home."

"They just left her there?" Ashley's hand

rose to her forehead, "and no one found her till morning?"

"I know. Bobby feels terrible," the sheriff said, "but by all accounts, it seems it was an honest mistake."

She felt guilty about her harsh tone, knowing that Mr. McCay would be a million times harder on himself. Her eyes were welling with tears.

"I know this is hard, but there's some things I need to ask you." Mueller hesitated. "Please understand, I've gotta ask these questions. It's my job."

Ashley wiped her eyes with her sleeve. "Okay."

"Now, by all accounts, Colleen was a healthy young lady, but who knows, it coulda been a heart attack or something." He placed his hand on her shoulder again. "Still, I gotta ask. You made the dessert, right?"

"What?" Ashley was confused by the question. What did she have to do with any of this?

Mueller grimaced. "They said all Colleen had to eat was dessert. And then—well, she got sick. I need to know what ingredients were in the cream puffs, and you need to confirm that you used proper food safety protocol to make them."

"What kind of question is that?" She could feel the heat rising up her chest into her neck. "Of course I did. I am trained by a world-renowned chef, you know. She's the best in the business."

She knew that it wasn't Mueller's fault, yet she couldn't help raising her voice. It didn't matter how good the food was; any murmurs of a sick guest could cripple a catering business, not to mention a baker's reputation. She took a deep breath.

"What I mean—what I mean is that my food safety standards are among the highest you'll find."

"Even so," said Mueller, "I just need to get this information in order to rule it out."

Ashley rattled off the recipe from memory. "Flour, eggs, butter, sugar—" You couldn't get any more basic than the standard pastry and cream filling recipe. The decorative flowers came from an organic grower, free of all pesticides and herbicides, and double washed with her own hands. It couldn't be her fault, could it?

"Did anyone else get sick? If it was only Colleen, it must have been something she'd had before."

"Darlin', I know, but we've got to rule out something contaminating the portion Colleen ate," Mueller said.

"Poisoning. You're talking about straight-up poisoning someone," Ashley said. "I don't make those kinds of mistakes, especially not with a partner like Patty, who's always gone above and beyond food safety standards."

Mueller put his hands up defensively. "I'm not sayin' you did. All I know is that the Texas heat can be fierce, and it's not always easy to

31

keep things at a cool temperature. If it was pois—uh, food-related—I'm sure there's a reasonable explanation. I'll call you if I find out anything else." He started to leave the room, then stopped.

"Now, I'm not going to release any information until we know something for sure, but you know how the people in this small town talk, and I can't help the fact that people saw Colleen eat your food and know that she got sick afterwards." He looked at her sympathetically. "I'll call you if we find out anything else.""

If they found out anything else. Mueller was nice enough, but Ashley'd seen enough sealed police records back when she dabbled in hacking as a teen to know that they didn't have the resources to handle anything more complicated than the odd speeding ticket or disorderly tourist. At least the state police were coming, but they had a habit of not taking small-town matters too seriously.

She went through the kitchen to the staff

bathroom, once again seeking its soothing powers. How was she going to explain all this to Patty, after she'd risked so much to relocate and take a chance on Ashley?

Staring at her blotchy face in the mirror sparked her memory of the previous night and the argument. Once she'd arrived home from the benefit and collapsed on her bed, the question of the identity of the man arguing with Colleen had nagged at her. It didn't seem important enough to give a lot of thought then but now? It could be a matter of life or death.

She continued to ponder as she went into the stall for a minute, then, saw a glint of something in the toilet, like someone had failed to flush it down—a smart-phone. Recognizing the Texas flag symbol on the case, she realized that she'd seen this phone before. It was the same one Colleen had been fidgeting with last night, except now the case and screen were smashed to smithereens.

If Colleen had died in the guests' bathroom,

what was her phone doing in the staff bathroom? And why had it also died such a violent death?

Ashley retrieved meat tongs and a baking pan from the kitchen so she could pull the phone out and lay it on the pan, making a mental note to retire them from cooking duty. She wondered if she should tell Mueller about it and the argument, even though she couldn't figure out who was yelling at Colleen.

Would trace evidence be lost from the phone after it was submerged? Would the police even bother with that, being the underequipped department that they were? More likely, they'd be satisfied with the conclusion that the dessert made Colleen sick, leaving Ashley looking guilty by association.

This phone, this beautiful broken phone, gave her hope that maybe there was a way out of this mess.

Handing it over without first saving the data herself, though, made her nervous. There had been a famously fumbled case a few years earlier- when the state crime lab accidentally lost data by overwriting it with their own files. At the very least, she could make a copy, as she couldn't imagine the state police would do a better job recovering the phone data than she could. She hid the phone between two pans, thinking that no matter how hard she tried, she could never escape the seduction of some exciting detective work after all.

When she got back to the car she realized that she'd left Dizzy, her faithful, loving, addle-headed dog, in the back seat. When she'd saved her from the pound, they'd told her that she was a "Bitsa. Bitsa this and bitsa that." She mostly looked like a Labrador crossed with a hound dog. Ashley had only intended to go inside briefly to get her trays, but Dizzy was still in her harness, sitting up, pricking her ears while licking her lips and staring at her intently.

"Oh, I'm sorry, Diz."

She put the trays on the seat next to the dog and gave her a scratch behind the ears before getting in and taking off for Fresh Start Kitchens, a shared commercial kitchen where she, Patty and other food entrepreneurs in the community rented space to do their food prep. Ashley dreamed of having her own store one day where she could sell her sweets, but for now, her baby Seagrass Sweets only did catering. It was the best option for her financially; she didn't have to take on a lot of risk with a store lease, but she could still bring in money and set aside some of her profit each month. Plus, she loved having space to share with Patty and others in the same business.

Her head was reeling from the news about Colleen and the possible poisoning. As she drove along the riverside on her way back to the kitchen, she felt two canine eyes tracking her thoughts.

Sure enough, when she looked into the rearview mirror, she saw Dizzy in the back seat, staring at her like a mother waiting for her child to confess. Ashley was taken aback with this new expression on her usually playful mug. She was quite the calm sage, in contrast to Ashley, who was doing her best to keep her frayed nerves in check.

"What? Why are you looking at me like that?"

Dizzy held her gaze for a moment before being distracted by a large truck rolling by. Her eyes soon drifted back to her mistress, who was studying her through the mirror. Ashley started to talk aloud, trying to assuage her own guilt and stop Dizzy from shaming her with that withering stare.

"I couldn't tell Old Man Mueller about her, Dizzy. I don't know anything about what happened. I mean, I heard Colleen threatening to expose a secret about Bobby McCay, but I have no idea what it was."

Dizzy had already disengaged and was now watching the people walking their dogs along the river. Ashley's mind was buzzing.

"On the other hand, what if Colleen's death was not an accident? What if it was," she shuddered in her seat, "murder? That could be dangerous. Should I have told Mueller what I know? What do I know? Nothing, that's what."

Chewing her lip, she glanced back at Dizzy again. The dog was now snoozing, the straps of her harness preventing her from slipping all the way off the seat.

Last night, after the successful event, Ashley felt on top of the world. It made her decision to move back home and open Seagrass Sweets seem like the right one, and she was finally starting to believe she could do this, build a life and a business in her hometown. But now? Trying to escape food poisoning rumors? She could see that dream crumbling around her. She had to do something.

"I know I could get Ryan to help—especially with the phone—and that email is the start of a trail of breadcrumbs that will lead somewhere.

Although, it could lead somewhere I don't want to go. It could lead to a killer."

She sighed as she turned into the parking lot of a large, non-descript warehouse whose bland exterior hid all the magic that happened inside at Fresh Start Kitchens. Dizzy was awake again and wagging her tail, waiting to be let out so she could sniff the perimeter of the property.

"Also," Ashley cringed at the thought she'd been silencing the whole ride, "what if it *was* my dessert that killed her? Oh, my God!"

Exasperated, she took one more glance at Dizzy, who quickly alternated from looking at her and the door. Her one-track mind wanted out. Ashley got out of the car and unstrapped Dizzy, who bounded out to begin her patrol while Ashley dragged the trays from the seat and made her way to the back door. She put Dizzy in the coat room, where she quickly found her doggie bed. Dizzy was not allowed in the actual kitchen, but Ashley hated to leave her at home alone. The coatroom was a nice compromise; it let Ashley check in on Dizzy frequently but did not offend Patty's high standards for cleanliness in the kitchen.

Patty came to greet Ashley at the door, holding it open with her left hand while her right hand wiped the flour from one rosy cheek.

"Oh, good, you found them." Patty nodded towards the pans.

Ashley walked through, still in a daze as her thoughts swirled in many different directions at once. Patty followed her to the kitchen, then took the trays from her young, frazzled friend and placed them on the counter.

"Penny for your thoughts?"

Ashley turned to face her. The tears were already flowing as she began to tell Patty the news. Patty held her hands while she spoke. When Ashley had finished, Patty wrapped her arms around her for a big, long hug.

"Honey, I am so sorry. I know Colleen was someone you knew, and no matter what other chaos has surrounded us, that fact is at the core of it all and it hurts." Ashley sobbed a few times into Patty's shoulder, then raised her head and wiped her tears.

"Honestly, Patty, I didn't know Colleen that well anymore. I'm sad for her family and friends, but I'm really most upset about what this could possibly mean for me, for you—for us." She looked away. "Does that make me a terrible person?"

"Honey, it makes you human." Patty held her at arm's length and squeezed her shoulders. "We'll be fine; we didn't come all the way from La Ville-Lumière to let the first little hiccup stop us." Then, being the pragmatist that she was, Patty began forming a plan. "What can we do first? We know it wasn't our food that did the poisoning, so we must try to determine what did. How long will the toxicology tests take?"

Ashley had to laugh at that. "In this town? Who knows if they even do toxicology tests?"

41

Patty's hopeful eyes dulled a bit. "But I do have an idea of what we can do," Ashley said. She pulled the phone out from between the trays. "Our first clue."

"Ooh la la," said Patty, grabbing at the silk scarf tied around her neck, "did you just say *our*?"

CHAPTER 3

AFTER CONVINCING PATTY that working on this mystery themselves was the best way forward to save their businesses, Ashley wasted no time in getting the phone to someone who might be able to bring it back to life. Dizzy grew excited as they approached Ryan's office, barking and whimpering, not even trying to contain herself.

"Okay, Diz, don't worry, we're here."

The dog barked her approval, and Ashley parked the car and texted Ryan to come downstairs for a surprise. Within moments, Ryan appeared at the front door wearing a huge grin and, like Dizzy, not trying at all to hide his excitement.

"Hey, Ash." He greeted her and opened his arms for Dizzy. "This is a nice surprise. To what do I owe the pleasure?"

While Ryan and Dizzy said hello, Ashley made her way up to them with a heavy heart. Ryan noticed straight away and stood up with a look of concern on his handsome face, his grin slowly disappearing.

"What's up?"

"I'm sorry, Ryan. I suppose you haven't heard about Colleen."

"Um, no. What?"

"Colleen's dead. They found her at the banquet hall."

"That was Colleen? My God. I saw a brief story in today's online paper about a death at the Women's Club; honestly, I assumed it was one of the 90-year-olds from the event. What happened?"

Ashley put on a brave face. "They're saying that she was poisoned. It could've been one of my desserts."

Ryan's eyes widened, and he opened up his mouth to say something before shutting it again. He gestured towards the door of the glass office building "Why don't you two come inside?"

The façade of the three-story building was made almost entirely of glass windows, and Ryan had the entire third floor for his business. Normally, Ashley would hesitate to bring Dizzy into a place so corporate looking, but she knew Ryan had instituted a dog-friendly workplace policy; being able to bring their dogs to work was one of the many things Ryan's staff loved about working for him.

Once they were inside Ryan's spacious office, Dizzy raced to the rawhide bone that was always in the corner, and Ashley threw herself on the sofa. Ryan made his way to the chair opposite her.

"I don't understand. Colleen was poisoned? That's hard to believe."

"Yes, and I'm horrified. You know how careful I am with food safety."

Ryan smiled. "Of course. All the time.

45

There's got to be more to the story, Ash."

"Well, that's why I'm here."

She dug the cell phone out of her purse and handed it to him. He turned the baggie over in his hands, fingering the pieces with a look of surprise.

"First of all, I assume this used to be a phone. Shouldn't the cops have it?"

Ashley gave a cheesy smile with a little shrug. "I would've handed it over to them if I thought they could do a better job, and I will hand it over to them—just after we, er, you make us a copy of what was on that phone."

Ryan sighed as he continued staring at the pieces. "So, you want me to see if I can extract data from this mess?"

"You're the only one I know who can find needles in electronic haystacks."

He smiled at her, then looked back down at the phone and frowned. "I don't know; I've come a long way from our black hat days. I had to leave hacking behind to build the company and," he gestured to the expansive ocean view outside of the window, "so far it's paid off."

"I understand, Ryan," Ashley said, "I shouldn't have asked. Risking your business to save mine doesn't seem like that great of an idea, now that I've said it out loud." She laughed quietly to herself. "I guess I just got caught up in the idea of it being like old times— you and me versus the Above-Grounders."

That made Ryan chuckle, and for the first time since Ashley handed him the bag, he started to open it. As he did, Ashley shifted uncomfortably in her seat. He peered into the bag and suddenly jerked his head back.

"I'm sorry, Ryan." said Ashley. "I should've warned you. I fished it out of the toilet."

"Yeah, no. That explains the stench."

They laughed as Ryan got up, taking the phone over to his computer. "I guess trying to salvage a broken phone for an old friend isn't a crime. I'll see what I can find but just this once."

He pointed toward the fridge.

"Can I get you a soda or something?"

"Yes, please. And thank you—for the phone."

"And can I get something for you, Mademoiselle?" Ryan bent down and scratched Dizzy behind the ears. He went over to the fridge, grabbed two sodas, a bottle of water, an empty bowl and a bag of chips. "What exactly are we looking for on the phone?"

While Ashley began telling him about the argument in the bathroom, Ryan emptied the bottle of water into the bowl and placed it on the floor next to Dizzy. Then, he ripped open the bag of chips and sat back down in his chair.

"The man and Colleen were arguing over an email, so I want to see what emails Colleen received recently. Also, the man said the email has nothing to do with 'us,' so I'm wondering if they were involved. As far as I know, Colleen was single, but maybe there are calls or texts to this mystery man." Ashley was getting excited by the prospects of finding something in that phone, and her eyes and smile starting to look a little giddy.

Ryan laughed. "Look at you. This really does remind me of our time in IT together– remember?"

"How can I forget? Before I even hit high school, my idea of Saturday night fun was hacking my neighbors' Wi-Fi networks and the library's firewall. I dreamed of an exciting career as a tech expert, decoding encrypted data, breaking into security camera networks, or whatever the secret agent on the other end of the line needed."

Ryan laughed so hard some chip crumbs sprayed from his mouth. "Was that what you found during our basement days at Smith-Corp?"

"Ha. Not exactly. But I found you—a kindred spirit. You and I had just had dreams way too big for that place." She thought about the day she resigned, not telling Ryan she wouldn't be coming back. She had meant to tell him all day but just couldn't find the words. She finally mustered the courage when they were in the parking lot at the end of the day when, out of nowhere, Sergey showed up to pick her up as a surprise. Instead of telling Ryan that she had quit and was moving to Paris, she just said, "See you later," and got into Sergey's car. She didn't see Ryan for two years.

"Do you think you'll ever come back to it?" Ryan asked.

Ashley smiled. "Nah, that life is over for me now. Plus, baking is more than a job—it's a passion—and I feel incredibly lucky to make a living doing it."

"Lucky for me, too, I get free pastries." Ryan patted his stomach for emphasis.

"Well, not totally free. I'm lucky to have you available when I need tech support." She gave him a playful punch in the arm and then stood up. "As much as I love taking this trip down memory lane, I've got work to do. Not only do I have real work—I'm catering a wedding tomorrow—but I have to find some time to talk to Hope. She and her father have always been close, so if Bobby has any secrets, she might know what they are."

CHAPTER 4

"ARE MY EYES deceiving me?" Hope asked excitedly. "Could it really be Ashley Adams?"

"I promise. I'm no vision." Ashley replied as she was scooped up in a friendly hug. She had walked to the McCay house down the same familiar route she had used countless times growing up. As usual, she found Hope sitting on her front porch, drinking iced tea and reading.

"It's been what, a bit more than three years since you went off chasing your dreams in exotic lands? Come, sit." They fell right back into their old routine, walking over to sit on the porch swing.

"If by exotic lands you mean sweaty kitchens, then, yeah. I'm sorry I haven't made it around yet. I haven't had too many free moments."

Hope had pulled her burgundy curls up into a messy bun. While other women are beautiful in the way that everything is just the right size and in just the right place, Hope McCay was beautiful in a way that no one else could possibly be, with a square jaw, a button nose and wide-set green eyes contrasted by her freckles. She was wearing a gold necklace with a pendant of a sea turtle that caught Ashley's eye.

"What a lovely necklace." Ashley complimented.

"Oh, thank you." said Hope. "My mom gave it to me, and I just adore it—it's so Seagrass, don't you think? Anyway, since I got it, I only take it off to shower."

"Hope, I wasn't sure when a good time would be to talk after—"

She hugged her grey cashmere wraparound sweater. "We don't blame you, Ash. I know you would never do anything negligent.

53

Dad would come down here and say it himself, but he's already done for the night."

Ashley felt a weight lift from her stomach, realizing that everyone who personally mattered to her was now on her side. Now the only ones left were the sheriff and Seagrass's entire event and tourism industry.

"How are you guys doing?" Ashley asked.

"It's just so sad," Hope said, staring off at the water. "Colleen was like family to us, being Dad's secretary for so long. I feel for Dad—he's in mourning, but he also has to figure out how to keep business going without Colleen."

Bobby McCay's primary business was real estate; he owned more of Seagrass than almost anyone. He started out when Ashley and Hope were young, buying up little parcels of land on the waterfront. Eventually, over time, he had acquired a huge part of Seagrass's shoreline. The Mouth, the estuary where the Colorado River meets the ocean tide, was his favorite parcel.

When they were younger, Ashley and Hope would kayak in the Mouth and the marshlands around it. After a long day of paddling, they'd eat dinner at the McCays' house, where Bobby would tell them the marshlands were "not only the beauty of Seagrass but the beast too," a fierce protector from flooding in hurricane season because they would absorb a lot of the excess storm water. Growing up with a father so protective of the natural environment, it was no wonder that Hope had made the speech she did at the banquet, calling for further protection of the natural beauty of Seagrass.

"Hope," said Ashley, "this may sound kind of strange, but I think there's something suspicious about Colleen's death."

Hope turned to her old friend. "What do you mean?"

"Well, for one thing, I know my baking didn't make her sick; someone must have tampered with the food."

Hope smiled at Ashley, then turned back to

face out into the yard again, avoiding Ashley's eyes. "Honey, no one blames you. Who knows how these things happen; but even huge businesses with millions of dollars can't stop it? I mean, look at Chipotle."

Trying to brush off the sting of being compared to a chain restaurant, Ashley continued. "It's not only that. I heard something that I wanted to ask you about."

"Go on."

"I was in the bathroom, and I overheard Colleen arguing with a man about an email that had a secret in it."

"Who was the man?"

"I don't know, but he was insisting Colleen keep the email a secret. And I think—I think the secret might have something to do with your father. Colleen said people would be shocked if they found out."

"My dad? What do you mean? What exactly did Colleen say?"

"She said, 'He's my boss. If people find out,

they'll be shocked.' And then the man told her not to be the one to tell people. This is a weird question to ask, but do you know of any secrets that your dad is keeping, and do you have any idea who the man trying to keep the secret quiet might be?"

Hope sat quietly for a minute before responding. She opened her mouth to speak a few times but didn't say anything.

"Please, Hope, can you think of anything? I am just trying to figure out what happened so I can clear my name. Anything?"

"Well, to be honest, there is something," said Hope, picking nervously at a hangnail on her left thumb. "My dad, well, he's been sick. He started to act really strange a few months ago, forgetting conversations we had and telling the same stories over and over again. At first, Mom and I just thought it was normal getting-old stuff, but then he would forget major stuff, like where he was or who we were. He'd always snap out of it, but it was alarming enough that we took him to the doctor. She says it's early signs of dementia, probably Alzheimer's. We had to come up with a quick plan, so I've taken on most of the responsibilities of his real estate business. Colleen was such a huge help with the day-to-day stuff."

"Hope, I'm so sorry. You know how much I love your dad." Ashley took a minute to let it all sink in. "And this was a secret?"

"You know my mom—she has to keep up appearances, so she just isn't ready to tell people yet. She thinks if people find out they'll start treating Dad differently and just make it progress faster. Of course, there's no medical research to back that up whatsoever, but who am I to disobey Mrs. McCay?" They both giggled at that—Hope's mom was always the strictest among their friends and the one they feared the most.

"Can you think of anyone who might want to keep that secret?" Ashley asked.

"No, not really. Maybe a business associate?

There's still a lot about Dad's business I don't know."

"Can you think of anyone who might have wanted Colleen dead? Or anyone sitting at your table that night?"

"Well, we've had some issues of minor vandalism." Hope lowered her voice as she glanced at the porch window. "I've been trying to keep it away from Dad to save him from any more stress."

"Do you know who's doing this?"

"Yeah, it's that crazy redneck gang that harasses anyone that ever wants to change anything around here. They call themselves the Localists, but they're just thugs with no vision for a future in Seagrass that looks any different from the past. They started messing around on our properties after they heard that Dad was considering selling land near the Mouth."

"Did you tell the sheriff about it?"

"Bah. That's a joke. He's not actually going around wreaking havoc himself, but Mueller agrees with them too much to do anything about it. He'd just tell them I complained, and it will fan the flames. I guess you get to do whatever you want if everyone in town loves you just because you're jovial and know how to smoke meat."

"Wait." Ashley said, stifling a laugh. "Are you saying that Smoke Daddy Lee is one of those cowboys?"

"One of them? He's the ringleader! It started with him coming down to the house every day, asking to talk to Dad again about how he's going to ruin this town. When Dad told Lee to stop coming around, we started finding little things broken or stolen here and there. Holes punched in kayaks. Busted floodlights. Then we discovered Dad's boat missing one morning and found it abandoned, floating around down river and totally trashed."

Hope stood up and began to pace across the porch.

"If they care so much about Seagrass, what

about us? We're locals, too. They've just gotten so consumed with their idea of the way they think Seagrass should be, they've forgotten how big a part of this town we've always been."

"So, you haven't actually seen Lee or anyone associated with his group doing this vandalizing?"

"I don't need to. It all started after someone saw Dad having coffee with a big hotel developer from Bayview Development. And then— if Colleen was murdered, that sure is a big coincidence. Most people knew she was one of Dad's most influential advisers, not to mention the fact that Colleen and Smoke Daddy Lee met several times before she met her maker."

Ashley made a mental note of Lee's and Colleen's meetings, even though she was shocked by the revelation.

"So you just have a feeling that it could have been them? Who else besides Lee do you think is involved?"

"Well, really, almost everyone in Seagrass

over the age of forty, but to narrow it down, Lee's lackeys that hang out at the Smoke-ground every day. All they have to do is walk down the path at night after they're done cramming their faces."

That didn't really narrow it down. Rednecks destroying property wasn't all that rare in Seagrass, so while Ashley was sympathetic to Hope, she didn't think there was much chance those guys were murderers. Honestly, they probably didn't have the brains to pull it off, even if they wanted to. Still, she made a note to ask around about the Localists to find out more.

"I hate to cut our reunion short, but it's getting late and I have some things to wrap up before the work day ends," Hope said.

"Of course," Ashley said, standing to give her a hug. "If you think of anything, would you let me know?"

"Of course, and if you figure out who that man was in the bathroom, let me know."

Ashley waved as she made her way down the front walkway, the long driveway and towards home. It was a lot to process. Even though Bobby McCay was possibly too ill to be conducting business, he seemed to be making a pretty big deal with Bayview Development. Maybe there was someone out there who would profit from revealing his illness to clients and partners, but who? That's what Ashley needed to find out next.

CHAPTER 5

EARLY THE NEXT morning, Ashley found Patty hard at work, peeling and deveining shrimp for that night's wedding event. She wondered out loud if it was even worth all the effort; most of the guests at the wedding would have heard the poisoning rumors and likely steer clear of their food.

"I guess you could always take the medieval approach to convincing people you're not a poisoner. Just go out there and start eating it in front of them, with relish." Patty stated, trying to make her friend feel a little better.

This wedding was just the kind of event they knew would be crucial to the success of their nascent businesses: a dreamy, beachside reception at the two-hundred year old Pleasant Inn, complete with a five-tiered wedding cake. Ashley spent all day baking and painstakingly decorating the cake with a gorgeous, rose swirl-patterned frosting and a decadent array of cream-cheese fruit tarts glistening with a sumptuous, drool-worthy glaze. She was happy to have a pleasant distraction. Slowly twirling the cake's turntable and using the frosting tips to create the tiny little roses was meditative, and she almost forgot her sorrows of late.

That didn't last long, however; no one touched the cake. After the bride and groom finished taking pictures cutting the cake, they put the knife down and scurried away from the table. The guests only picked sparingly at Patty's shrimp linguine, which, despite her brave face, Ashley knew upset her. No one said anything aloud, but Patty and Ashley both knew it had been too late for the newlyweds to cancel, and they had still wanted nice-looking food in the background of the photos. Ashley kept apologizing to Patty for the poisoning clouding her catering business by proxy. Patty continued to shush her and tell her that it wasn't her fault. Both of them watched with horror as multiple guests snacked from food they had carried in their handbags to keep from going hungry.

It had been two full business days, but so far, the state police hadn't detected any signs of toxins in the leftover cream puffs from the benefit, and their kitchen had passed the inspection. Ashley was allowed to operate, pending the test results of Colleen's stomach contents, and the investigation was still ongoing, just like the whispers behind Ashley's back.

She was annoyed that, after all that work she'd done to be accepted, her business could be facing closure. Seagrass locals weren't your typical southerners. They didn't all come installed with that famous southern hospitality. The tension between established residents and

The disruption of tourism development had hardened the locals (whose families, like Ashley's, had lived there longer than Texas had even been a state) to outsiders.

When Ashley made her homecoming after two years in Paris, she did so with peace offerings of blood orange cupcakes and bags of Patty's truffle oil popcorn. This, along with approval from Smoke Daddy Lee, the King of Texas Barbecue and purveyor of local attitudes, helped her and Patty start building a reputation as the town's first caterers of fine French cuisine and desserts. Luckily, Lee's approval of The Southern Bird had survived the cream puff fiasco, as his birthday party dessert order was the only other booking that hadn't cancelled yet.

As the wedding guests were drunkenly dancing to bad 90's pop music, Patty and Ashley finished cleaning the kitchen and escaped to the stock room to play cards and gossip with the dining room staff. There was something about eating out that made guests forget service staff wasn't deaf to private conversations or that their waiters and bussers could take these secrets with them after their shift. Most Seagrass dining room staffers took shifts at venues all over town, so if one kitchen knew something, they all did.

After Ashley collected a carefully selected team of busybodies, it only took one round of Rummy in uncomfortable silence before she realized that, for once, they had nothing to dish. All the juicy tidbits they'd overheard were about Ashley.

"Okay." Ashley dropped her cards on the table. "Just go ahead and ask me."

She'd barely finished her sentence before Sabine Clemons, a usually timid teenaged busser who had recently reinvented herself with a nose stud and dyed-red tips in her light brown hair, exhaled with relief, as if holding her breath had been the only thing keeping the words from escaping.

"You couldn't have made a mistake like that, right? That's what I keep tellin' people—I say there's no one more careful about what goes in food than Ashley."

"I've been sayin' the exact same thing." Mark Griffin joined in. He was a graying, seasonal waiter who only picked up shifts when the fishing wasn't good. Thanks to his ever-present hat tan, Mark always looked like he was wearing a pale, mismatched, bald cap.

Across the table, Patty smirked at Ashley with one of her poor attempts at covertly sharing a pointed look. After enduring so many years of over-eager flattery from wannabe-protégé chefs, Patty had no tolerance for yes-men. Being "too afraid of her kicks to kiss her feet" was what initially earned Ashley her approval. As smooth as Ashley wanted Patty's transition into Seagrass to be, it sure was fun to watch her ruthless, but somehow playful, cynicism mix with the country folk.

Maude Nehls, the dining room manager,

was impatiently tapping her foot, hungry for Ashley's scoop. She always pulled her tortoise-shell glasses slightly down the bridge of her nose when she sniffed privileged info in the air, her middle-aged gossipmonger senses tingling. If you wanted to spread word fast, Maude was the most infectious patient-zero.

"There's just no way," Ashley stated. "I keep going over it and over it in my head. I know I did everything by the book. Everyone ate the same ingredients, but no one else got sick. The symptoms appeared too soon to be food poisoning, and it doesn't really make sense for a fatal dose of E. coli or norovirus to accidentally fall on one exact portion unnoticed, right?"

"Unless someone brought something like a syringe of poison to directly inject into the cream puff," said Maude, adding quickly, "oh, I suppose I read too many murder mysteries."

Mark gasped. "No, that's what I thought, too. I was like—wow—you could really squeeze some poison in one of those puffers!"

The table murmured thoughtfully, and Ashley saw Patty's eyes light up with excitement while she fingered the silk scarf she had tied around her neck. Unlike Patty, Ashley understood service industry social politics well enough to know that, when it came to initiating this kind of information extraction, it was better to avoid coming out directly and asking questions. Not that Ashley's side of the story was particularly shocking, but an expert busybody was more likely to reveal their hard-earned commodity if it felt more like an exchange of goods. She had to incite intrigue by delicately tipping over the pot and directing the conversation with her own hesitant spillage; then, the small-town gossips wouldn't be able to resist tipping until they had spilled the whole dish.

Watching Sabine purse her lips, Ashley knew she'd have something. "Ya know, Mark and I worked that banquet. The McCays' table got riled up from all directions that night even before Colleen got sick."

Mark nodded. "Yeah, I told Sabine. Remember, Sabine? When we brought out the dessert wine, I said, 'Something going on with Bobby. He looks sick and tired.'"

Sabine laughed. "Bobby looked tired until Emma Phee sauntered over, running her fingers up and down his arm while asking him how he liked the food."

"That's right," Mark replied. "That kept him happy until his wife came back from the bathroom and Emma left, giving Colleen the evil eye."

"The evil eye?" Ashley asked. "Why?"

Mark smiled slyly. "Turf wars, I suppose. Emma Phee is an eligible bachelorette, but I think Colleen had already filled the vacancy. Bobby is getting pretty old, you know. One mistress is probably enough."

"What?" said Ashley. "Colleen and Bobby were having an affair?"

Mark raised an eyebrow. "You didn't hear it

from me, doll."

"I didn't even notice all that," said Maude. "I was just on the lookout for that ole mister Monty big shot. He was watching the McCay table all night, and I was just waiting to see why, see if he'd go over there." Maude was chewing her soda straw and wearing a far-off look.

"Monty? How do I know that name?" Ashley asked.

"Oh, Monty Gahn," Maude replied, peeking over her glasses for emphasis. "He's that mineral rights broker trying to get his hands on every natural gas deposit on the Gulf Coast."

Sabine giggled. "Wearin' a bolo tie, snakeskin boots and a cowboy hat, like he's tryin' to be some cheesy oil tycoon villain. Lived in Texas all my life, and I've never even seen anyone dressed like that before."

This was the man Ashley had been hearing so much grumbling about since she'd returned to town. The Seagrass community was so protective of its local character, even talks of building new hotels over four stories tall could cause an uproar. When this outsider came around hoping to drill into the natural beauty that Seagrassians held so dear, Ashley was surprised that they hadn't chased him out with torches and pitchforks.

"And if hassling property owners wasn't enough, I heard he's trying to settle down here in Seagrass—even tried to buy a parcel in the marshland, right next to the McCays' Mouth," said Maude. "But I can't imagine Bobby was having any of it; that piece of land is priceless."

"Oh, darling, everything has its price." Mark leaned forward and lowered his voice to a near whisper. "I heard Bobby was selling the Mouth to a hotel developer, Bayview Development, from Houston. Maybe old Bolo Tie is a sore loser."

"Probably why Colleen steered Monty over to the corner of the room. Didn't wanna stress out Mr. McCay," Sabine remarked. "Poor Colleen.

Being the personal secretary to Bobby McCay couldn't have been easy, but I never woulda guessed it'd get her killed."

Maude flashed a smile. "Colleen was pretty unassuming, but she could be fierce when she needed to be. After she talked to him, Gahn got outta there quick. You know," she added, gesturing with the ace of spades for emphasis, "if I was going to poison someone, I wouldn't stick around long after."

"Oh, yeah," Mark said, crossing his arms, "you'd get outta there."

Leaning over the table, Maude lowered her voice. "You know, honey, you might be on to something."

"You think Monty Gahn might have killed Colleen?" Ashley asked. "What would be his motive?"

"That guy's a creep who doesn't like taking no for an answer. Colleen believed in protecting the marshlands just as much as Bobby—maybe he got sick of her telling him he couldn't buy the land to drill."

That seemed far-fetched but, then again, so was a murder in quiet Seagrass. Ashley needed to find out more about who this Monty Gahn character was and what exactly his business with Bobby McCay involved.

"Any news about the phone?" Ashley asked.

"Oh, you mean the one you stole from the dead lady?" asked Ryan.

"First of all, I didn't steal it," said Ashley, "I found it. Second of all, Colleen had a name. I'm just not used to the idea that she's—well, let's just call her Colleen, OK?"

Ryan looked a bit startled by her response. "Of course, Ash, I'm sorry."

Just then, Dizzy bumbled up to Ryan, trying unsuccessfully to climb up his legs to sit on his lap. They both laughed, which cleared the tension in the room.

"I love that she still wants to be a lap dog," said Ashley. "I'm glad our years in France didn't turn her into a refined dog."

"A visit from you would have been enough, but bringing her derpy face to butter me up for news about the phone didn't hurt either," Ryan stated, swiveling his chair back and forth as he rubbed his dark stubble, pretending to ponder. "You know, it wasn't that long ago that you were on this side of the desk, complaining about all the friends and family that came to you with their crumb-clogged keyboards and shattered touch screens. Now you come and drop a cracked toilet phone into my hands."

Ashley was secretly thrilled with the idea that Ryan liked her visits. She placed a bow-topped Tupperware container next to his "bang head here" mouse pad. "But wait, there's more. I'm offering brown-butter, chocolate chip cookies too."

Ryan sobered. "I haven't had time to touch the phone yet. You know, it's not too late to just give the police the phone. Won't messing with it make any evidence inadmissible anyway?"

"You know as well as I do that we are not messing with the original data. Just copy the SD card data and the internal memory card onto fresh cards and then mess with those. And not just that email, her pictures, texts, or whatever else we can recover. It could tell us more about what's going on."

Dizzy turned in circles over Ryan's feet like she always did before dizzily plopping down. It was a habit which had earned her the name. Ryan nodded; Ashley knew that he'd get the phone data for her and that she wouldn't have to ask again.

"Listen, I'm catering Smoke Daddy Lee's Birthday Bash at the Smokeground this afternoon. Can I convince you to sneak out of work a few hours early and join us?" she asked.

"Are you kidding me? My mouth is just watering at the mention of it, like one of Pavlov's dogs." At that comment, Dizzy barked and jumped up, making them laugh again.

"Great, why don't you meet us there in a little while? Maybe after you've copied the SD cards?" She knew she was pushing her luck with Ryan, but she also knew he'd say yes.

Ashley crossed the street with Dizzy in front of Ryan's office to get to her car, parked next to a green-space where they had stopped to let Dizzy chase squirrels before going in to see Ryan. She had to let her burn out some of her infinite energy or an office visit could be a disaster. Just as Ashley opened the back door to let Dizzy jump in, the dog saw a bunny on the other side of the park and made a mad dash for it, somehow seizing the exact moment that Ashley had put down her leash. "Dizzy! You silly mutt, get back here!"

When Ashley finally caught Dizzy and was heading back to the car, a jogger ran by on the path and nearly right into them. It was Emma Phee, local socialite extraordinaire. She balked at Dizzy's enthusiastic jumps at her feet and snapped at Ashley.

"Would you mind?" Recognizing Ashley, she calmed down and back-pedaled. "Oh, hello." Her tone, though civil, was haughty.

"Hey, Emma. Dizzy—back off!" She pulled Dizzy back to her side. "How are you?"

Emma regarded her with slight disdain mixed with what seemed to be pity and courtesy.

"Wonderful, and you?"

Ashley was nervous about Emma taking a dig at her about the cream puff fiasco, but her mouth took over before she could think.

"Great—thanks for asking—although I'm still trying to come to terms with Colleen's death."

Emma tilted her head and nodded, still with her nose in the air. "Yes, it's awful, isn't it? But you know what the good Lord says, you reap what you sow."

For a moment, Ashley was so shocked at Emma's lack of sympathy for the dead that she didn't know what to say. Emma gazed at Ashley with a look that hinted slightly at baiting a trap, and Ashley took the bait. "How do you mean?"

"Well, it's not like me to speak ill of the dead, but rumor has it that Ms. Colleen was doing more than just secretarial work for Bobby, if you know what I mean." Ashley honestly didn't know. She waited, hoping it would become obvious.

Emma could wait no longer. "They were having an affair."

Dizzy was tugging on the leash, anxious to keep moving, but Ashley felt like she had been given a great gift, the gift of information from someone who had been giving Colleen the evil eye the night of her death. Give a little, take a lot. That's how it usually went with the gossipy types.

"Yes, I've heard that too," she said. "I also heard about a suspicious email. One of the wait staff mentioned that they overheard an argument in the bathroom—between Colleen and a man!"

Emma's reaction was not what Ashley would've expected. Her eyes widened and she started blabbering.

"Well—yes—but who knows what that argument was about? It probably had nothing to do with her death. Besides, Colleen wasn't as sweet and innocent as everyone makes out." She stopped blathering as quickly as she'd started, like there was a voice in her head reminding her not to say too much. "I'm sure the police have it all under control." She breezed past Ashley as she began to make her way to her car.

"Nice to see you Ashley. Good luck with your business." Emma started jogging again and, after only a few strides, was too far away to hear a goodbye.

Ashley was taken aback. It wasn't just the smirk on Emma's face when she'd wished her good luck, it was the way she'd responded to the conversation about Colleen. Maybe Colleen and Bobby had been having an affair and

Emma was jealous. And what did she mean by "not as sweet and innocent as everyone makes out"?

Before she could ruminate any further, Dizzy jerked forward and began dragging her back toward the car and the smoked meat that was in their future.

CHAPTER 6

"HURRY! PUT THE fork down, Patty, before someone sees you." Ashley stage whispered, looking around at the other tables in mock alarm.

Before its bed and breakfast revitalization, people only knew the name Seagrass for two reasons: fishing and the Smokeground. Tourists still didn't consider their trip complete without getting a taste of Smoke Daddy Lee's famous Texas brisket and ribs, but for the locals it was practically a religious experience, and eating barbeque ribs with a fork was the number one mortal sin.

Patty scoffed and dropped her plastic fork in

disgust. "You know, I really do respect this whole barbeque thing—as I do any artfully crafted roast—but if you're going to make something messy and sticky, let a girl have her fork."

Seeing Patty in shorts for the first time was like the surreal feeling one would get seeing their high school principal in swim trunks. Not only did she seem much less intimidating (and shorter) without her chef hat, but Ashley was still not accustomed to seeing Patty in civilian clothes. After seeing her "pit-bull in the kitchen" persona every day in the restaurant, it was easy to forget that she actually possessed a delicate, petite frame.

Patty studied her ribs carefully, which was her standard evaluation procedure for any new dish she thought could be worthy of praise.

"Think of all the time spent wiping your mouth between every single bite, inelegant and inefficient."

Ashley felt a familiar comfort in knowing

that—shorts or not—there was no setting casual enough for Patty to abandon her culinary etiquette militarism.

"Well, yeah, we're not savages," Ashley replied as she grabbed another wet napkin from the tabletop dispenser. "Besides, everyone knows ribs taste better straight off the bone."

She really didn't expect Patty to fully embrace the spirit of Seagrass's favorite watering hole. Smoke Daddy Lee had always defiantly preserved the original setup of his oak tree-shaded riverfront oasis, consisting of: a pull-behind smoker latched to a food truck, a herd of wooden picnic tables covered with disposable tablecloths and Uncle Bertrand as the front of house manager, who could always found sitting in his polyester folding chair to accept cash-box payments and scare tourists with his tall tales.

As Ashley breathed in the scent of burning hickory and applewood, she thought of all the nights she'd spent sitting on the Smokeground dock as a kid, dangling her feet in the river as she ate off a paper plate in her lap. It was a simple pleasure that hadn't worn off as she got older.

Carefully avoiding contact with the habanero lime barbeque sauce, Patty picked up her ribs by the very edge of the bones, slowly tugging them apart. Dizzy was sitting upright on the bench watching her every move and ready to pounce on any falling scraps.

Patty took a small, thoughtful bite. "Hmm." She followed with one slow nod, the rarely witnessed Sign of Patty Approval. "Tender. Pulls clean off the bone without totally falling apart— and still juicy—even after all those hours in the smoker." She looked over at the adjoining campground, packed with tents and RVs for the Smokeground Campout. "No wonder people camp here just to watch Lee cook."

Every Saturday, meat smoking started early in the morning and went late into the night. Eventually, locals developed the tradition of setting up camp to eat all day, killing time between each meal napping, fishing the river and playing horseshoes. If that wasn't gluttonous enough, some campers set up shop on Friday for the Smokeground Eve Cookout, where Bertrand and Lee cooked over an open campfire.

Camping spots for Lee's free birthday Smokeground Campout were so coveted that he held a raffle, which required a chopped wood donation for entry. Everyone always knew what time of year it was when you could hear the echoes of axes thumping all throughout the area.

So, it was obvious why it was such a big deal when Lee didn't cancel his monster order of Ashley's treats.

"Either they don't realize that I made the desserts or our plastic distraction ploy is working," Ashley stated, noticing the crowded dessert table.

They'd bought a bunch of the plastic containers used by supermarket bakeries, "sealing" them with a piece of clear tape around the rim. Patty had tried to argue that it would protect against Dizzy's shedding and "dirty camping germs" before admitting that it would make people feel more "comfortable."

As someone who didn't bake with poisoning in mind, Ashley thought that it looked a little defensive.

"It probably has more to do with Lee's tastemaking skills than anything. He's like a hillbilly hipster," Patty laughed.

Lee was working the grill, his recently-budded bald spot glistening with sweat under the glow of the string lights, with a spatula in one hand and a maple-bacon, bourbon cupcake in the other. Throughout the day, he'd amassed a pile of cupcake containers on the nearby hammock, otherwise known as the "Smoker's Throne." His grey, breast-pocketed t-shirt, the only style of shirt he owned, was smeared with a rainbow of Ashley's cupcake frosting. It was probably going to be the next hot new look for the men of Seagrass in their early forties.

Ashley heard a familiar voice behind her. "Wow, this triple chocolate cupcake's plastic box makes me feel so safe and secure. It is definitely uncontaminated." A sunburned, bedraggled Ryan fell onto the bench next to her.

"Shush. We're doing so well." Patty waved a rib bone at him threateningly. "It's good to see you're alive, though. After you disappeared, I worried the Cult of Barbeque used you as a human sacrifice."

"Don't make me laugh," he said, wincing. "I got drowsy after eating too much brisket and accidentally fell asleep in the sun."

"Oh, that's actually my fault," Ashley quipped. "Back at the kitchen, Lee let me inject the meat marinade. Probably why it was so delicious."

The Smokeground went through far too much meat to store in its food truck, so Lee also rented space in Fresh Start Kitchens.

Dizzy ducked under the table, sniffing at Ryan's front pocket.

"Hey, girl, you found the drives." He greeted Dizzy with a pat.

Back in the IT basement, they'd trained Dizzy to find things that they regularly misplaced, like their keys and flash drives. Now that she didn't get to play as much, she "found" similar items without prompting.

"Thanks for reminding me. I'm not sure how long it will be before my mind and body give out. So, we have some 'technology' to talk about."

"Oh, that sounds serious." Patty gave Ashley a cheeky look, like she was a tween with her first-ever date to the dance. "I need to go practice this whole networking thing again, anyway." She pulled her cheat-sheet of names she'd been memorizing from her pocket and headed towards the campground. Then, she twitched her shoulders, shifted her head, opened her palm, raised both eyebrows and made an audible raspberry. Ashley could hear the "je ne sais pas" in her mind that almost always follwed this Gallic shrug.

Ryan raised his eyebrows, which made him wince again due to his sunburn.

"You're sending her out to win over the townsfolk?"

Ashley shrugged. "When we were abroad, she could really turn up the charm if she had to. The social dynamics are practically inversed. Americans use a lot of words to say hardly anything at all, and they find French bluntness rude. The French speak more precisely, getting right to the point and find American rambling exhausting. Even I struggled to readjust here."

"At least her English is amazing. She doesn't even have an accent."

She started laughing mid-sip and choked on her soda, making a frantic grab for napkins as she felt it coming up her nose. She knew that it had been suspiciously long since she'd made a fool of herself. At least she managed to smother the situation before things became airborne.

Ryan grinned. "You need some air, Ash?"

"Nope, found it." Her face felt redder than his looked. "The thing is, I'd hoped that she'd be good with English, seeing how she was born and raised in New York. Americans tend to assume she's French, though."

"Huh?" He looked puzzled. "French way of carrying herself, I guess."

"Yeah, but it sounds like she's always been that way, and Europe just suited Patty. I did warn her that Southerners can find people who don't want to express their every thought and emotion as rude, but she's a homebody anyway, so it doesn't seem to bother her much."

His face grew a little more serious. "You think she's happy here?"

"I don't know. I don't hear about her hanging around anyone outside of work, but she likes the country tranquility compared to the city, although she values her privacy and alone-time, so it's not crazy to think she'd like it here. Why?"

"Oh, it's nothing. I was just thinking how big of a risk she took, giving up everything to move somewhere she'd never been."

"Just because she's socially reserved doesn't mean she's not brave. Besides, she's a world-famous chef. It's not like she can't pick up where she left off. I'm the one getting my big break."

Ryan smiled. "Speaking of business, let's get down to it." He pulled a memory card storage case from his pocket, sliding it across the table like it was a back alley deal. "Your copy."

"Have you gotten anything from them yet?"

"Yeah, actually, there were two files downloaded from an email two days before Colleen died, and I've been able to recover one of them so far." He paused and gazed downriver. "The file contained the results of a geological survey for the McCays' property, the kind you would do before selling."

Ashley sighed. "So the McCays are selling off part of their huge property. Why is that so scandalous?"

"Maybe the McCays wanted to keep it a secret for the sake of negotiations, and the man was trying to protect Bobby's interest in the deal?"

"Or maybe it was about who they were selling to. Monty Gahn was looking to buy a piece of property on the marshland—maybe they were making a deal. And my kitchen gossips told me he and Colleen had an argument the night of her death."

"Gahn," said Ryan. "He's that guy who wants to mine natural gas deposits all over town, right? That can't be a coincidence."

"C'mon, don't make me ask," Ashley said. "OK, fine—what can't be a coincidence?"

"The survey was different than most. It covered the whole property, but the focus was the location of shale gas deposits lying underneath it."

"Well, that in itself is not that surprising. Most of the surrounding lands have those gas deposits underneath them. That's what brings guys like Monty Gahn to town."

"Yes, but no one has ever sold land to be mined, so most land purchase deals wouldn't even have such a survey done. People are too afraid to be the first to allow such mining in Seagrass—fracking is still very much a curse word here. The fact that someone conducted the survey recently means that it's suddenly become relevant, maybe because Bobby is considering selling."

Ashley shook her head. "Bobby's put his heart and soul into that land. I just can't see him selling land to anyone who wasn't interested in preserving it. Like you said, not one person in Seagrass has ever allowed gas deposits on their property to be extracted. Unless..."

She hesitated to tell Ryan about Bobby's illness because Hope was a friend, and it felt like betrayal to share her secret. "Unless Gahn is trying to take advantage of Bobby now that he has Alzheimer's."

"Could be," Ryan said so nonchalantly that Ashley was confused.

"You know about Bobby?"

"Well, you know this town. Secrets don't last long."

Even though she had grown up here, she had been away long enough that she sometimes forgot just how tight a community it was.

"Maybe Gahn found out about Bobby and was trying to get him to agree to a deal that he normally wouldn't have," Ryan said, "and Colleen was getting in the way."

"But, then, why Colleen?" Ashley asked. "I'd certainly like to know what she and Monty were arguing about at the banquet, but I'm not convinced that file is anything more than a work-related document and we might be chasing down the wrong path. Let's see what that second file is before we jump to any conclusions about Gahn. In the meantime, I need to think of a way to learn more about Emma Phee. She was giving Colleen dirty looks at the banquet. I just ran into her on the way over here, and she was acting really suspiciously."

CHAPTER 7

AFTER A DAY of introspection and cleaning up her finances, which were showing the effects of the repercussions from Colleen's death, Ashley was relieved to be spending the evening with family. Even though there was no immediate danger of financial ruin, she was concerned about how things would turn out if business continued to slide into a slump. Her brother Michael was a great cook and listener; she could always count on him to cheer her up and talk some sense into her.

In order to curtail the throbbing headache which loomed on the horizon, she'd drawn a bath complete with essential oils and candles, after having a cup of chamomile tea and making a batch of cinnamon pecan cookies. She sighed as she pulled into her brother's driveway and wondered how she was going to solve the case and pick up the pieces.

Once she parked and let Dizzy out, Michael appeared on the doorstep, laughing when Dizzy suddenly stopped her inspection of the azaleas and barked excitedly before racing up the steps and leaping into his arms. Ashley had noticed more than once how her dog seemed to appreciate males far more than females. Even though Michael was a big guy, he struggled to contain Dizzy's exuberant bulk. He finally put the dog down, rushing over to Ashley and giving her a huge hug.

"Hey, Sis. You smell purdy." he teased.

She laughed and pushed him back as she passed the tub of cookies to him. "Here, silly-pants."

He didn't wait to crack the container open and take a deep sniff. "Oh, my favorite!"

Ashley followed Michael and Dizzy into his rustic house. Her brother had already started scarfing down a cookie, rolling his eyes in a comical show of pleasure.

"Mmmm—oh my God!" he exclaimed, "what a perfect marriage—pecans and cinnamon."

Ashley laughed and shook her head. She'd always enjoyed his skills with amateur dramatics and his ability to describe her cooking in such an enthusiastic way. She sat down on the overstuffed sofa while Dizzy went from room to room on her usual inspection route. Michael brought a glass of lemonade for her and sat on the other end of the sofa with the tub of cookies on his lap.

"I hope you don't expect me to share these with you," he said with mock seriousness.

"No, big brother, they're all for you. I wouldn't dream of depriving you."

"I don't even care if I spoil my appetite for dinner, which I'm sure you'll find boring in comparison to your culinary superiority."

"Oh, don't be ridiculous." She sniffed the air with a grin. "What is that? Roast chicken?"

He sighed in defeat and hung his head

101

sheepishly. "You know me so well. It's the only thing I can make that could be considered half decent."

She nudged him playfully with her foot. "Come on, Mikey, you're a great cook."

"Yeah? Well, you're my sister, you have to say that." He winked as he took a huge bite from yet another cookie.

"And I mean it," she responded as she began twirling her hair around a finger.

Michael watched her for a moment. "Okay, what's wrong?"

"Nothing. Why?"

He gave her his signature look when confronted with one of her vague attempts at covering up her true feelings, his hazel eyes wide open while his eyebrows hitched upwards and his head tilted to the right. She smiled through gritted teeth before slumping in her seat and sighing loudly. She'd never been able to pull anything over her brother.

"Oh, just the whole poisoning affair, Colleen's death and my business being on the brink." She knew that it sounded melodramatic.

Michael put the lid on the tub and placed it on the coffee table. As he brushed the crumbs off his sweater, he gave his sister a steady look.

"Sounds pretty bad, but that's not the sister I know."

"Really? What sister are you talking about? Because that girl sounds like someone from a long time ago."

"Actually, she sounds like a few other female relatives who are always down in the dumps and blaming everyone else but themselves."

Ashley pouted and crossed her arms. "I'm not like them."

She did not like being compared to their mother or their aunt, who had always been quite depressing and negative.

"I know. I remember someone more like

Nancy Drew than Negative Nelly," he quipped with a wink.

"Who's Negative Nelly?" she asked, smiling in spite of herself.

"At the moment—you." He laughed and got up from the sofa, motioning for her to follow him to the kitchen. "Come on, let's eat."

They continued talking while setting the table and plating up.

"I have been doing my own little investigation," she confessed.

"Thatta girl. Tell me more."

She told him all about the argument she overheard, finding the geological survey with Ryan's help and rumors of Colleen and Bobby's affair.

"What do you know about mining shale gas deposits?" She could always rely on her brother's encyclopedic knowledge on just about anything.

"What, fracking? Well, it's a contested topic here in Seagrass, that's for sure. Basically, we're sitting on a gold mine of natural gas that is really hard to access. One way to get to it is hydraulic fracturing—or fracking—where they shoot high-pressure fluid into the earth, causing breaks in the rock bed that the gas can flow through. When they can get to that gas, well—ca-ching!"

He took a bite, chewed and continued. "On one hand, fracking brings jobs and money to the local economy. But, on the other hand, there are a lot of environmental impacts. Scientists at UT-Austin say that most of the earthquakes we feel here are because of fracking. Plus, there's all the industrial infrastructure they have to build. I have a buddy who lives up near Cotulla—he says the lights from the wells and mining equipment make it hard to see the stars anymore at night."

"I was gone when this became such a hot-button issue," she said. "What do most people here in Seagrass think?"

"Depends who you ask. Lot of folks who've

been looking for work would love to see it come to Seagrass but most are fiercely against it. The damage it would cause puts at risk the tranquility and natural habitats that draw in the tourists. I reckon the biggest deposits are in the marshlands; that's a pretty fragile area."

"Yes, the McCays' marshlands, right? I suppose they are not too tempted by the money, given they're one of the more well-off families here in town."

"If they were, the Localists certainly would make it difficult for them to give in to temptation."

"Yeah, Hope was telling me about these Localists—she says they've been vandalizing her property. Who are they?" Ashley asked.

"Oh, it's a bunch of guys around town who are trying to keep Seagrass from changing. Standing against progress, if you ask me. I heard the McCays' trouble with them doesn't even stem for fracking, just for considering a sale of land near the Mouth to a hotel developer. I respect a person for taking a stand, but these Localists are too cowardly to reveal who they are, and they go around destroying property of hard-working people. It just makes me mad."

"Do you know anything about a Monty Gahn?"

"Gahn, yeah, I've heard the name. He arrived a few months back, trying to get people with property to let him mine on it. But like I said, no one has yet. In fact, I think he's earned himself the nickname Mother Fracker, which tells you how people feel about him."

"Well, Gahn was seen arguing with Colleen the night she died. One of my theories is that he was trying to take advantage of Bobby's declining health and manipulate him into selling. Maybe Colleen got in the way?"

"Could be, Ash," said Michael. "You know, I hope you're being careful. These Localists are hooligans, and nobody knows much about

Gahn. I hate to think you're putting yourself in danger."

"Awww, my brother," she teased, "just like on the playground as kids when you'd beat up anyone who bullied me."

"Still, it's not the same as when we were kids." He smiled reassuringly. "Well, your detective instincts might be the same."

Ashley laughed and nodded. "Oh my God— remember that time we tried to solve the case of the chicken heart?"

He pretended to shudder. "How could I forget? When Mrs. Jackson came running into our yard and showed it to me, I was disgusted."

"She was always a strange old woman, but showing that heart—with the thorns sticking out—to two teenagers while screaming like a banshee? Too much."

"I couldn't get over the fact that she was trying to blame it on Mom. What a nut."

Ashley shrugged. "Well, they never got along, but she didn't get along with anyone."

Michael smiled. "It was fun checking out all the facts. I got so excited when her husband told us that she dabbled in Strega witchcraft."

"Yes, and remember the librarian's face when we asked her if they had any books on Italian magic?"

He burst out laughing. "Oh, yeah. When she asked, 'What are you two up to? You wanna put a spell on someone?' I wanted to say yes."

Ashley smiled. "The most exciting thing for me was when we realized Mrs. Jackson put the heart in the mailbox herself—just for attention—then she tried to blame Mom."

"It was the same deal with the dog turd three months earlier, remember? Dad saw her scoop it up from the sidewalk and shove it into her own mailbox. I laughed so hard when he called her a looney nut-job."

"How could I forget? That's how we put two and two together."

Michael took a sip of juice and leaned back in his chair. "That was a lot of fun."

Ashley took another mouthful of stuffing and pointed her fork at her brother. He frowned.

"What?"

She swallowed. "So, it was okay for me to be a sleuth back then but not now, when my livelihood is being threatened?"

"Well, this is a little different, Sis. It's not a simple case of dog turds or chicken hearts stuffed in the mailbox."

"I know that, but I don't want to risk losing what I've worked so hard for. All that studying, perfecting my recipes and growing the business—it's all at stake here."

Michael put his hand on her shoulder to reassure her. "Okay, just promise me that you'll play it safe."

"I will. Besides, I have Ryan helping me."

"Ah, yes—Ryan." He smirked.

"What? What does that mean?"

"Nothing, but I know you have feelings for him. I think you have for a long time."

"You're so wrong, Michael. He's just my friend."

"Yes, but you said the same thing about Serge, remember?"

Ashley shuddered at the mention of his name but didn't respond.

"Is that still a sore point?"

She pondered the question while she played with her food. She had tried to block out those memories over the past few years. It wasn't just the pain of the breakup but the idea that she had been used as a pawn in his dangerous hacking exploits.

"You know how I feel about him and that time in my life." She paused before going on, suddenly losing her appetite. "Even though I'm over him now, I'm still angry that I fell for him. I should've known that his charm and good looks were too good to be true."

"You were young and impressionable. Don't be so hard on yourself. Besides, at least you got away from him before the blowback hit you."

She sighed heavily. "True, but I should've seen the signs. Now there's still that thought in the back of my head that it could come back to bite me."

"What do you mean?"

"You know, he could still come back to seek revenge. I had to clear my name and tell the truth. He had me breaking the law with what I thought was routine IT security work for paying clients." She took a moment to take a deep breath and stay calm. "I wasn't going to take the fall for him, so I told the investigators everything I knew. If I'd helped him, he'd now be living in the lap of luxury on some remote island. Instead, he's running from the authorities and trying to stay under the radar. Seriously, he could turn up at any time."

Michael shook his head. "You know you've got your big brother to look out for you." Trying to joke to alleviate the stress she was obviously trying to hide, he added, "And Ryan, maybe even Patty—and Diz."

Dizzy came running over, always in tune with any mention of her name, even when abbreviated. Michael scratched her under the chin and tossed a bean in the air, which she expertly caught and swallowed in zero time.

Ashley smiled. "That's true—and comforting—but I still keep looking over my shoulder."

Michael got up and began to clear the table. "Well, you know what would help you feel safer?"

"A tougher dog?"

"Come on. Dizzy worships the ground you walk on, don't you, Diz?"

Tail wagging lazily, Dizzy followed him into the kitchen. Ashley got up to help. Michael turned to face her while leaning against the counter.

"Don't you think it's time to settle down, Ash? Find yourself a man to love—someone who truly loves you and will take care of you."

"Oh, my God! Stop channeling Mom." She

groaned and slumped her shoulders for emphasis.

"OK, OK." He looked at her in such a kind way, her heart swelled a little bit. "I just think you deserve someone who respects you and has nothing but good intentions."

It felt too silly to cry, so instead Ashley punched his arm. "Look who's talking. When are you going to settle down, now that we're on the subject?"

Michael adopted a macho stance, puffing out his chest. "I'm a playboy, baby! I'm in my prime."

She shook her head emphatically. "Decline, baby, not prime."

He rushed over and grabbed her in a headlock, giving her a noogie while she screamed and pummeled his legs.

"Stop it, you mongrel. STOP!"

Dizzy began to bark and leap up on Michael, so he decided to let his sister go. She slapped him across the head, and he pretended to kick her while holding the dog at bay.

"See? Dizzy's got your back."

Ashley bent down and grabbed the dog in a frenzied hug, making her even more excited. Michael went over and started to pour the coffee while Ashley collected herself and told Dizzy to calm down.

"I'm serious, Ash. You do need to find someone who really cares about you. I know that you like to project an aura of independence and stability, but I can see the loneliness in you."

Ashley was well aware that no one knew her better than Michael, but she stubbornly shook her head. "Thanks for caring, Mikey, but I'm fine."

"What about Ryan? He's such a great friend and you two have always been close, even when you went to Paris. You know, he often called and asked how you were while you were away?"

This secretly pleased Ashley, but she maintained a tough exterior. "So? He had my email address. He could've asked me himself."

115

"Maybe he's shy? You know, it's getting harder and harder these days for men to approach and talk to women. Who knows how he really feels?" He paused, and then added as an afterthought, "Hey, if you like, I could do some detective work on your behalf."

Ashley grinned at his enthusiasm.

"Sure. You want to help with the case?"

Michael's smile quickly evaporated, followed by a playful groan.

"No, silly, I meant—talk to Ryan on your behalf. I could find out how he really feels about you and report back. It could be the beginning of a beautiful relationship."

Ashley grabbed a wooden spoon from the counter and pretended to threaten her brother.

"If you do, it'll be curtains for you, see? I'll put you six feet underground; is that understood?"

CHAPTER 8

THE SEAGRASS POLICE station didn't exactly evoke images of law and order. Located in a re-modeled schoolhouse, complete with wooden panels which were painted streetlight-yellow, it was known for the meticulous maintenance of the luxuriant oleander bushes out front. Ashley had come to turn over the phone. Now that Ryan had copied the SD card and all the data from the phone for them to try and recover, there was no purpose in obstructing justice any longer.

Before Ashley reached the front steps, Mueller's voice hollered from the bushes; then he crawled out backwards, feet first. Trying not to giggle, Ashley thought, "The amount of time our boys in blue spend with their hands gardening in the dirt shows what a small threat crime is in this town."

The sheriff squinted up at her. "Ashley. I've been hopin' to give you a call sometime soon!"

"Do you have news?"

"Oh, no. I was just hopin' to. What brings ya here?"

"I might have some news of my own, actually."

"Really?" He sat cross-legged, patting the grass next to him. "Take a seat. Our grass is the best seat in town, promise."

She sat, knowing that the lawn received more grooming than Dizzy did.

"You remember how I came to pick up my pans that morning after Colleen died?"

"Sure. I about had a heart attack thinkin' we had an intruder at the scene of our death investigation." He wiped sweat off his brow with the back of his hand, leaving a thin line of dirt across his forehead.

"Well, you know, I haven't been cooking a lot lately, seeing as how people are afraid that my food will kill them, so I just got around to washing my pans. I'd left them sitting in the oven at the venue, but when I unstacked them at home, this was lying between the pans."

Technically, it wasn't a lie. She pulled a zip lock bag holding Colleen's reassembled phone from her purse. "And I recognized it as Colleen's phone."

"It was missin' all this time? How'd it get in the oven in your pans?"

"It looks like someone tried to destroy or hide it, and there are signs of water damage, too." Again, not a lie. "I once worked in IT, you know."

"Seems like too big of a coincidence, her dyin' the same night her phone is assaulted and drowned."

She didn't necessarily think of Mueller as a bad investigator, he was just never afforded the opportunity for much practice. The biggest mystery in Seagrass had been the time Bertrand lost his prize hog on the riverbed, and it turned out to be sleeping in the mud under another hog. It would be natural to think that the best explanation was the least sinister one.

"That's what I'm thinking. I brought it down right away for you to keep as evidence."

"Looky here, now. This kind of turn in the case is good for you. Here I was hopin' to call you with good news soon, and now you call upon me with your own good news."

"Yeah, life is funny that way, I guess."

She decided to hold off telling him about Colleen's argument with the unknown man, unless it became necessary. She was growing more frustrated each day that she couldn't figure out who the man was.

"It came at a good time, too. They're runnin' test after test for all the toxins fitting her symptoms but so far, no matches. So it's gotta be somethin' uncommon, but they gotta know what they're testin' for, first."

"So, if they used some crazy obscure poison, the lab might never confirm what it is?" Ashley's heart sank. She and her business couldn't afford any loose ends that might still leave room for suspicion at the end of all of this.

Mueller stretched back against the grass, propped up on his elbows and stared up at the clouds. "They're lookin' at the molecular structure and whatnot right now, but there's a limited amount of time and resources they can spend on a case with no other evidence of foul play. But I think you could have just brought in an extension."

"Just doing what I can to help. Colleen was a friend of mine, so I want to know for closure's sake. Is there anything else I can do?"

"Nah, hon, you're good. I wish all Colleen's so-called friends were as good-hearted as you." Mueller shook his head and looked down at the phone in his hands. "Can you believe that

Emma Phee was just down here yesterday, asking if she could get back a bracelet she lent to Colleen? She actually had the gall to ask us to let her look through the victim's purse, if you can believe that!"

The hair on Ashley's arms prickled. That was the second time she'd heard a strange story about Emma Phee's behavior since the murder. She knew that the woman had enough money, so she didn't have to steal from Colleen, but what could she possibly have wanted in that purse?

"Hey, I was curious about something, Sheriff. Have you heard anything about any vandalism or harassment of the McCays lately?"

"I heard 'bout it but not from them." Mueller's lips pressed into a thin line. "I wish people would ask for my help more, but 'round here, people like to take care of their own business. They think callin' the police would be makin' too much of a fuss." He glanced around the garden. "I mean, not like we got much else to do."

"What do you think about plans for a big hotel at the Mouth?"

"If I had my way, not much would change. Except maybe my usefulness." He chuckled. "I suppose a big hotel would require a larger police presence. Lots of domestic disputes at hotels. But the McCays have kept greedy hands off the Mouth for a long time without any profit to show for it, so if they wanna sell, we shouldn't give 'em a hard time for it."

Ashley guessed that if Mueller was sympathetic to the Localist movement and had reason to think they had something to do with Colleen's death, he'd know better than to talk about it with someone close to the McCays. If this kind of extremist talk was going around, it wasn't going to be out in the idyllic, landscaped yards in broad daylight. She needed to find the kind of place it did happen, but Seagrass didn't exactly have a designated seedy underbelly.

She wished people were as easy to hack as

computers were. Just then, she felt her phone vibrate in her pocket, pulled it out and read a new text from Ryan.

"Stop by office when you can—new development on phone."

"On my way," she texted back, giddy with anticipation about what the new development might be.

In the car, Dizzy watched intently for her return. Ashley got in and turned to scratch her head.

"What is it, girl? Feel like a visit to your favorite IT guy?"

Even though she knew that Dizzy was a dog, certain words seemed to trigger a response. She didn't even have to mention Ryan's name. Saying "IT" made the dog prick up her ears. She barked and began panting excitedly.

"Okay." Ashley laughed and drove off.

"Well," Ashley said as she walked into Ryan's office, "what is the news?"

"Hello to you too." From the look on his face,

she could see he was not put off by her direct-
ness but rather proud of himself for his discov-
ery. "See for yourself. I pulled a few photos from
Colleen's phone."

He turned his laptop around and Ashley sat
down. She gasped as she scrolled through several pictures of Emma Phee and Bobby McCay
arriving at and leaving different hotels and res-
taurants—as well as at the McCay property,
walking in the garden.

She looked up at Ryan. "Emma told me that
Colleen and Bobby were having an affair; that
seems awfully suspicious given what we know
now. What else is she hiding?"

"What do you mean?"

"Sheriff Mueller just told me that Emma had
asked him if she could get something from Colleen's handbag. It could have been these photos, or it could have been evidence of the murder. Now that we know what she and Bobby
were up to, I want to hear it from her mouth.

Then I'll be able to see for myself if she's a murderer too."

Ryan was nodding thoughtfully as he followed her train of thought and jumped a little when his cell phone rang from the other side of the room. He was too slow to get to the call before they hung up, so he called voice mail while holding up his palm to Ashley.

"Forgive me a second, I had several client emergencies today, so I just have to check these." He put his phone on speaker, turned the volume way up and starting typing on his computer while listening. The first message was from his mother, reminding him of his niece's upcoming birthday. The second was from a client, talking about his SSL certificate being expired and unable to process any credit card transactions. Ashley felt intrusive hearing the messages, but there was no way to avoid it.

The third message started as though the caller thought Ryan had actually answered.

"Hey broooo," slurred the man's voice.

"Whassup?" A long pause followed until the man realized his mistake and started laughing. "Ok, dude, I get it, you're not there. But when you get this, you gotta come out right noooooow. That girl I was telling you about is here and she is hooooooot."

The message continued, but Ashley stopped listening. She heard the sound of her own pulse in her head and little else. Set up with a girl? It was silly, but she never really thought about Ryan having a social life. She just always pictured him at work or at home or with her. The image of him out at a bar, talking to a girl, drinking and flirting, popped in her mind and she couldn't think of much else.

"Sorry about that," Ryan said. "That was a drunk dial from Eddie last weekend from a bar, trying to set me up with some girl he knew from work."

Ashley snapped back to the moment. "Wait a minute—Eddie? Your old friend Eddie?"

"Yeah. Now that he's engaged, he's been

127

trying to set me up with all the hot girls he wishes he could date. I save his messages for comedic value." Ryan shook his head to get back on track.

"That's him—that's the voice!" exclaimed Ashley.

Ryan looked perplexed.

"That's the voice of the man that I heard arguing with Colleen in the bathroom the night she died."

"Eddie was arguing with Colleen? Are you sure?"

"100 percent." She jumped up and began to pace back and forth.

"If you think it was Eddie, what was that argument all about?" Ryan asked.

"I don't know. I always thought that Eddie's temper was bound to get him into trouble sooner or later, but could he murder someone?"

"There's only one way to find out."

"I guess we are going to talk to Eddie," she said.

CHAPTER 9

THEY HIKED DOWNRIVER to where Eddie parked his RV, where Ryan had been a few times with the guys for poker night.

"Remind me about what you heard in the bathroom again," Ryan said. "I want to be sure we're on the same page."

"Eddie said something about proprietary information in an email he didn't want Colleen to release. Now we know that might be this survey file, but it might be the other file we haven't accessed yet. Then it sounded like there could have been something—you know—between Eddie and Colleen. I'm not sure exactly what it all meant, but it was more than a fight about business. You said Eddie is engaged, to whom?"

"To Hope. I assumed you already knew that."

"Really? I mean, I've only seen Hope the one time since being back, but you think an engagement would be something worth mentioning. How strange."

"I'm curious, though," Ryan said. "Besides the argument, is there another reason you might be a little quick to suspect Eddie? Maybe something to do with a long-lost pigtail?"

"Oh, so he told you about his elementary school reign-of-terror. I mean, it shows you the kind of cruelty he's capable of," Ashley replied, only half-kidding.

"You've got to understand, Eddie has this inability to interact normally with females. You'll see." He knocked on the door.

"Oh, hello, dog," Eddie said as he waved Ryan, Dizzy, and Ashley into his luxury RV, which was bigger than most Parisian apartments. "Ryan, my man, it's been too long. You keep bailing on me for guys' nights out. If I let you use my bathroom, does it mean you'll come out this weekend?"

Ashley was quick to interrupt. "I'm the one who has to use the bathroom, and all it means is I'd rather use your glamper toilet than the port-o-potties at the Smokeground, nothing to do with guys' nights out."

Eddie flashed his bright smile, which was something Ashley had come to know as his most persuasive feature. He brushed his disheveled, glossy, black hair off his forehead and continued to grin.

"Ha-ha. Ryan did say you were still a huge tease."

Ryan's eyes grew wide. "He means that I said we tease each other. Like, playfully. A back and forth," he stated emphatically, glancing nervously at Ashley.

131

She was preoccupied with checking out Eddie's RV on her way to the bathroom and didn't notice. The RV was fairly clean and organized, but fairly full of stuff for a temporary dwelling—things like laundry folded in three full baskets along the wall and clean dishes filling the kitchen shelves and stacked along the counter. He also seemed to be using the kitchen booth table as a work desk, with piles of paperwork surrounding his laptop. Was he living out of his RV, she wondered? He wasn't the kind of guy who would choose to live like this permanently, and he could definitely afford a place of his own.

Once in the bathroom, she set her smartphone camera to panorama and arranged it so that the camera lens peeked out from her cross-shoulder satchel. She wouldn't have been surprised if most of Eddie's passwords consisted of his birthday or Hope's middle name, but people also commonly chose passwords related to the things surrounding them. She decided that pictures of his living space might come in handy for their snooping.

When she returned to the lounge area, the men were in full swing.

"And I'm telling you, Ry, this thing had to have been thirteen feet at least. Oh, Ashley, have you heard the story about that gator snapping at me a couple weeks ago?"

"Uh, no. We don't talk, Eddie." It came out a bit harsher than she intended. She knew that she needed to at least pretend to be interested in catching up with him.

Eddie shrugged. "You could have still heard about it." He sat on the couch, propping his feet up on a laundry basket.

"Huh. Around here, that's actually true." She said, pretending to admire the RV's features as she walked through the living space, trying to get a variety of angles for her camera.

"He was with Monty Gahn," Ryan said pointedly.

Dizzy joined him in the now-cramped booth, taking the whole length of the seat as she lay across his lap.

"Oh, yeah." Eddie's voice dropped as he gave Ashley a deer-in-the-headlights look. "I know people around here really hate him, but he's not that bad of guy once you get to know him."

She decided not to take his word for it. "Where did you see the alligator?"

"Oh, I don't remember."

"Bufort, right? You just told me that," Ryan said, amused.

"Right. Hey, Ashley, I know Hope has been talking about wanting to see you now that you're back. You should go over and say hello."

"I did see her, just the other day."

Eddie averted his eyes. "Oh, I guess she didn't mention it. How are you holding up after everything?" When Ashley looked at him blankly, he added, "You were the caterer who..."

"Who did what? Baked a cream puff that

was later dosed with something poisonous?"

His mouth fell open with surprise. It might have been riskier to take the more confrontational route, but at the very least, she knew they might get something from his reactions. Not that this one gave away much. If he had nothing to do with it, the statement could still surprise him.

"Did you know Colleen well?"

"Not really, she just worked for Bobby."

Ashley wondered why he would downplay Colleen's significance to the McCays. Even if Colleen and Eddie hadn't really been close, everyone knew that she meant more to the family than just an employee.

"Oh, I could have sworn I heard you talking the night she died like you were close."

She saw something flash across his face but it wasn't panic. Was it relief?

Ryan was visibly focused on petting Dizzy, looking really uncomfortable. She didn't blame him for not participating.

"I could have sworn I overheard you guys arguing." She laughed, pretending that it was all a harmless misunderstanding. "I've been curious, were you guys fighting about something?" She smiled playfully.

"Sorry, I just don't want to talk about this."

"Oh, okay. Should I ask Hope when I go see her, like you suggested?"

Eddie's face slowly shifted into an upturned smile, while Ryan shot her a warning look.

"Well, she's the one who doesn't want me to talk about it. But since you obviously already know so much, she probably wouldn't care if I told you."

Ashley nodded innocently and continued to secretly scan the area.

"Colleen had snooped through my emails. She was worked up over a project that I've been working on. If you've heard the rumors, you'll know why I don't want anyone to know about it. It's a proposed hotel project at the Mouth, a big development that some folks will call an

136

eyesore. The company that made an offer to Bobby, Bayview Development, said they'll hire my company to build the hotel if the deal goes through."

Ashley glanced at Ryan, who seemed just as confused as she was. If this was the truth, they were way off.

"And Colleen didn't like the idea of a big hotel, like everyone else?"

"Not exactly. She had come up with this harebrained money-making scheme. She wanted me to tip off Bayview about the shale deposits so they could buy the whole property, drop the hotel plans and make way more money extracting the gas. Her plan was that I'd negotiate a cut of the fracking business in exchange for the tip-off. Of course, that's not how any of that actually works, but she had it in her mind that we'd take the money and run off into the sunset together."

Ashley gasped at the last sentence; she

hadn't expected him to broach the subject unprompted.

"Because you—"

Eddie seemed to be ashamed. "I was sleeping with her. Yes."

Ashley remembered what Colleen had said. "It has a lot to do with our future here in Seagrass," and "He's my boss." Maybe she had been talking about not being able to stay in Seagrass if they betrayed Hope.

"Before you go and mouth off to Hope, Ashley, she already knows all of this. Colleen threatened to tell Hope if I didn't go along with her insane idea, so I did what I always do. I went straight to Hope and told her myself—brought her flowers—and now we're working it out. Like we always do."

"And that's why you're living out of your RV."

"Yeah, if you want to wring-out every drop of my humiliation."

"When did you tell Hope about the affair?"

asked Ryan.

Eddie seemed surprised to see Ryan was still there. "Right after the argument with Colleen. I needed to get to Hope before Colleen could; it was my only chance to do the right thing."

More like to cover your ass, Ashley thought. That would explain why Hope didn't mention the engagement to her; if she had just found out about Eddie's affair with Colleen, maybe she wasn't sure the engagement was still on.

"People saw Colleen arguing with Monty Gahn that night. Do you know what it was about?" she asked.

"I imagine she was telling him to be patient, that the mining rights would be his in due time. Getting Gahn to back off so she could lure in Bayview was all part of her plan."

"Theoretically, if someone poisoned Colleen on purpose, do you have any idea who would do that?"

"The only answer would be those crazy Localists. Most people know Bobby's sick, so they assumed that Colleen was making most of the decisions on his behalf. The hotel development probably pissed off those goons enough to do something stupid. I guess in that way..." He looked down at his feet, unable to continue. "I guess in that way her death is my fault. I really wanted that hotel project."

Eddie sat silently, holding his face in his hands. His back started to move up and down, a sure sign of silent sobbing.

"Maybe we should go," Ryan said, patting Dizzy to get up and giving Ashley a look that told her to agree.

"Yeah. You should." Eddie got up, his face wet with tears, and stormed into the back bedroom, slamming the door behind him.

Dizzy lagged behind, sniffing excitedly at the couch cushion. On a whim, Ashley quickly slipped her hand between the cushions. Surprised with her find, she smuggled what felt like a flash drive into her pocket, then left the RV and caught up with Ryan as he made his way up the path along the river.

"Well, Eddie's side of the story makes sense in most ways. It also proves my theory of Eddie being a jerk but not a murderer," Ryan stated, as the crickets began to herald the sunset.

"Yeah. Basically, he was trying to keep a profitable, but controversial, job on the down-low. But the part about Colleen wanting him to double-cross Bobby and secretly sell the mining rights to the land, that seems like a stretch."

"You think it sounds out of character?"

"For the Colleen I knew ten years ago, yes, it seems out of character. She was such a staunch environmentalist, I can't imagine her wanting to profit from a company mining in such fragile land as the Mouth. But who knows? People change."

"And people do strange things for love," he mused.

"Do you think Hope could have killed Colleen after finding out about the affair?"

"If Colleen had been bludgeoned to death, Hope would be my number-one suspect. But Colleen was poisoned—that requires premeditation and time to plan."

"Let's assume Eddie is telling the truth; Colleen wanted to tell Bayview about the shale deposits and use the money to run off together. That makes sense given what I heard in the bathroom. It also takes Gahn off the suspect list."

"But adds the Localists, whoever they are," Ryan said.

"And if we assume Eddie is not telling the truth...well, let's just add him to the suspect list for good measure."

"You know, I didn't think Eddie was that bad. All that, 'I told Hope and bought her flowers and kept on being a scumbag like I always do,' or whatever. I've never heard him talk like that."

"Sounds like he charmed you, too." Ashley teased.

"Yeah, that's why I feel way less guilty now about the keylogger I installed on his laptop when I was alone in the RV."

She expected to see Ryan smiling mischievously, but he was staring blankly at the river. She knew that suspecting your friend of murder was hard to stomach.

CHAPTER 10

"THAT'S RIGHT, GIRL. Now, you gotta give it some love. Tell it, 'thicken up, buttercup,'" Lee said while overseeing Ashley stirring his award-winning rib sauce.

"Thicken up, buttercup!" she exclaimed.

If Lee was in the Fresh Start Kitchens when Ashley was around, he would agree to be her barbecue sensei if she helped him with the prep work. Ashley was relieved to be back in the kitchen. She and Patty had a few jobs that people hadn't cancelled, most likely because they had been scheduled well in advance and it was too late to get a new caterer. But Ashley wasn't going to let that bother her; she loved having work to keep her busy. That night, they were just cooking in a private home for a couple's anniversary dinner, but at least they were getting paid well for it.

She finished baking her scrumptious, chocolate molten lava cakes while Patty was working on her own rich sauce for the macaroni Béchamel. Even though it needed time to simmer uninterrupted, Patty would hover over it protectively. She loathed other chefs touching her food unless it was absolutely necessary.

Other barbecue cooks would have stabbed someone with their grill fork to protect their secret recipe, but Lee's was public knowledge, as its secret had "nothin' about what you put in it, an' ever'thang to do with who is puttin' it in." Surprisingly, Lee's style of cooking was mostly guided by spirit.

"See, right now, it just lost its last baby tooth. You wanna let it simmer 'til it's ready to leave momma's house." Lee advised, peering over the pot.

"Oh, so that's what I've been missing."

"Woo, Patty. You gotta smart tongue on this

one." Lee hollered.

The kitchen was set up with rows of identical island counters, each paired with a top–of–the-line set of appliances and storage pantry. Smoke Daddy Lee, Patty and Ashley were neighbors.

"I know," Patty replied, shaking her head as she chopped basil with lightning speed. "It's a plucky one, that tongue. Surviving all this time around sharp knives."

He leaned back on the counter and wiped his already clean hands on his apron. "You didn' bring that dog of yours that's always followin' you round? Piggy? Squishy?"

Patty gasped. "Never. To think."

Ashley always washed and stored her uniform in the commercial kitchen and then showered every time before entering the cooking area. Dizzy's black fur did have an evolved survival instinct, so she understood the concern.

"I observe a cleansing ritual of Dizzy's hair

before I step into any kitchen. So it goes without saying that Dizzy definitely stays home."

"Aw, that's too bad. I like her. She sits on my picnic benches like she's a person. Most dogs act like animals in a place so thick with the smell o' meat."

Lee glanced over at The Southern Bird kitchen space, which Ashley felt he'd been doing a lot more than usual. Was she just being overly paranoid now that she had murder on her mind? In any case, she was glad that she had a camera aimed at their pantry now. As much as she didn't want to believe that anyone—especially Lee—would tamper with their stock, a lot of things had been happening lately that she wouldn't have believed.

"Why you got such a long face today, Ashley? Better crack a smile before it hits the ground." He grinned at Patty. "We all know that wouldn' be sanitary."

"I, uh, was just thinking about Colleen. You know, I hung around the McCays a lot growing

147

up. So—"

"Oh, darlin'. I'm sorry, what a shock it is," he said, scratching his coarse, black goatee.

"Did you know her?"

"Oh, yeah. E'rbody did. She and the McCays came down the road to eat all the time."

"But they don't come around anymore?"

"Well, you know. Bobby gets too tired to go out much now, so Hope stopped showin' up, too. And Colleen was busier helpin' out more. But I bring over a big ol' helpin' every time Bobby gives me a call."

That didn't sound like a guy harassing the McCays, but Lee wasn't exactly specific about when these welcomed visits were happening. Ashley decided to go for broke, even though her heart wasn't in it—she knew that she had to take the opportunity to get whatever she could out of him. If he was innocent, she could help clear his name, but if he was guilty? She didn't even want to think about it, even if it meant clearing her own name.

"Hey, Lee, tell me this, I'm just curious, did you have any dealings with Colleen—business or otherwise?"

He seemed a little shocked as he looked over her shoulder.

"What's that you say? Oh, business? Sure!" He splashed a dash of vinegar into the pot. "If I can recollect properly, we met two times: once when ol' Bobby wanted yours truly to cater a private event and the other was...let's see now." His eyes sparked up as he continued. "Oh yeah—that's right—when Bobby went on a private fishin' jaunt. He asked me to cook for him and his guests."

Before Ashley could respond, Patty jumped in, just as Ryan entered the kitchen and waved on his way to the back room.

"Lee, I heard you were thinking about starting your own catering business. Is that true?"

Lee's eyes darted around nervously, and he stammered, "Um, uh...maybe."

Patty became animated. "That's wonderful,

but you're not thinking of trying to run us girls out of town, are you?"

She winked at Ashley, who was becoming annoyed at the interruption. She stirred so hard that she splashed herself with a little of the sauce. Lee seemed to be too lost in thought to notice.

"Uh, nah, come on, girl. You and Ashley are untouchable, right? Besides, the Smokeground is my main concern. I never really thought 'bout catering until ol' Bobby brought it up."

Patty smiled sweetly at him. "Well, if you ever change your mind, we'd be happy to help in any way. Right, Ashley?"

"Sure." Ashley did her best to fake enthusiasm. The last thing she needed while her business was in jeopardy was competition from the local food hero.

Visibly relaxing, Lee leaned over the sauce. "How's it look? Is our boy ready to leave the nest? Hmmm. I think it's out of high school, but he needs to get a job and save up a little first.

It should be done by the time I get outta the john." He took off his apron and hurried away.

"Well, that was weird," Ashley said.

Patty tasted her sauce with satisfaction. "He's a guy who's chosen to be called 'Smoke Daddy.' I've never even called my actual father 'Daddy.' No way he's of the average sort."

Ashley wondered if he could be the murdering sort. He didn't seem like he had any anger toward Colleen, but why did he up and leave in such a hurry? What was he trying to hide?

"Hey-yo," said a familiar voice at the kitchen door. "Smells amazing in here."

"Hello, Ryan," Patty said. "What brings you to our kitchen?"

"I came to talk to Ashley about something, but now that I've smelled the wonderful aroma in here, I've come to offer my services as a taste tester."

Ashley smiled, untied her apron and hung it up before Patty could even respond. "Work first, taste second. What do you have for me?

151

Any news to tell me?"

"Well, yeah. If you can spare some time, it'd be easier to show you at my office."

As they walked into Ryan's office, he led Ashley to a new desk in the back corner. "Welcome to Surveillance Central." Ryan had gone all out arranging their "snoop cave"—fully utilizing his firm's spare equipment—so they could watch from the point-of-view of their "persons and places of interest" cameras.

"In seeing it now, through your eyes, I may have gone a tad overboard," he said, "but never mind that. So far I have two feeds to watch—Eddie's webcam and the surveillance cameras from the night of the banquet. I'm still trying to crack the password for the banquet's archive footage."

"May I?" Ashley asked, walking over to the keyboard. He nodded and she tried a few passwords until, on the fourth try, she guessed correctly.

"PASSWORD123. That's the password."

"You're kidding me," he said, rubbing his eyes under his glasses. She thought the glasses made him more appealing, but he only used them after looking at a screen for so long that his contacts dried out.

"These guys sound like they need a good IT consultant. Does 'Hello, I hacked your security and want you to hire me' work as an introduction?" she teased.

"You would be surprised how many clients I've gotten that way." He nudged her to move over and started typing and clicking on the computer.

"Oh, good, looks like they store footage on the cloud for thirty days," he said as he started to download all the footage from the day of Colleen's death.

Unfortunately—but not surprisingly—there wasn't a camera in the dining room. Ashley guessed that not many crimes occurred in the middle of fine-dining parties packed with people, but it did turn out to be the perfect setting to poison someone, apparently, completely unnoticed.

"At least we can see who is going in and out." Ryan took a sip from a liter of orange soda.

Venues like the Gulf Coast Women's Club were concerned with monitoring their parking lots full of expensive cars, their combined worth in the millions. Besides, a security camera would look terribly unfashionable in the middle of all that upscale décor. People wanted safety measures, like security cameras, but not the visible reminders that the world needed them.

While Ryan tried to find the footage from the banquet, Ashley looked at the screen that had the view from Eddie's hacked webcam. Eddie hadn't even bothered to change his factory security settings, meaning that his webcam could be accessed by anyone willing to spend a few hours online learning how to hack it.

Onscreen, Eddie had been reading business news on his laptop for the past 30 minutes when he suddenly sat up and started touching all his pockets—first the breast pocket on his shirt, then his pants' front pockets and finally stood up to feel the back pockets of his pants. When he didn't find what he was looking for, he started feeling around between the couch cushions, eventually tossing each of them across the room, getting progressively angrier with each toss.

"Whoa. He is not happy," Ryan said. "I wonder what he's looking for."

"Oh, yeah." Ashley reached into her purse and pulled out the flash drive, which was a heavy duty kind fitted with protective rubber padding. "Probably this."

Ryan grinned mischievously. "And where did you find that?"

"Dizzy found it. All I did was move it into my pocket."

"So, you stole it?" Ryan accused, still grinning.

"I didn't say that. I said I just moved it into

my pocket." She turned the drive over in her hands. "Why in the world do you think Eddie would need a padlocked and encrypted flash drive? For all his close gator encounters?"

"You know, one of my clients is a construction company, and sometimes I see people who bring computer equipment out to construction sites use drives with rubber padding like that. Other times, that level of security is required by a company to comply with insurance requirements."

Ashley groaned dramatically, spinning around in her desk chair. "And if Eddie's been telling the truth, it could be initial construction plans for the hotel, and this is his hapless attempt to prevent the Localists' sabotage."

She was surprised to find that Eddie had picked a decent padlock combination, as all variations of relevant birthdates didn't work. If it was a four-digit code, it was almost always a birthday.

"Tsk-tsk. He goes through all that trouble

to fortify a flash drive but doesn't even bother to secure the camera that watches him in his own home. Why do I feel like breaking this encryption is going to be a huge bother, only to find out that it's just the blueprints for his dream man cave?"

Ryan's hotel footage had finished downloading, so he called her over and they looked at the security camera viewpoints: front door, service staff door, two side doors and parking lot. They started with the service staff door, only because the one thing she knew for sure was that someone had disposed of the phone in the bathroom close by it.

"Whatever it is, I guess I'll know it when I see it," she stated, fast forwarding through a stream of service staff arriving. The footage showed her and Patty getting a good workout going back and forth loading their equipment and prepped food from the van. On the last trip, they recruited an athletic looking waiter to bring in the cake box which held the croquembouche. She didn't see anyone "sinister" hiding in the shadows, stalking the cream puffs for the perfect time to pounce. Frustrated, Ashley wondered why it couldn't be that easy.

"There's a window here, out of view of any camera, where the cake box was alone in the van, but that's not a lot of time to complete the tampering. And no way to control who eats the bad puff." She opened another bag of chips from their snack stash. "But if it's the kind of plot where any random target would do, why just one? Wouldn't someone being treacherous just for treachery's sake want to be a little more dramatic?"

Ryan shrugged. "Well, if one poisoned person accomplishes their goal, maybe they don't want to do any more damage or draw more attention than they have to. What if they just wanted someone to get sick but gave them too large of a dose? Colleen couldn't have been more than a hundred pounds soaking wet. Maybe the poisoner used a dose calculated to make someone on the heavier-end sick enough, but unluckily, it was a fatal one for someone Colleen's size."

"Oh, wow!" Ashley exclaimed. "You've already put a lot of thought into this. So why would someone do that? To make someone look...oh, right." She sighed. "To make someone look bad."

"Or some business look bad."

"What? You mean, Patty and me?"

She'd been so fixated on the idea that she'd been framed for negligence to cover up a murder, she'd never considered someone framing her for negligence to make her look, well, negligent. She wondered why anyone would do that.

"If someone was going all this way to hurt Patty, they would have bothered to sabotage her food, and I don't exactly have any enemies. I just moved back to town and spend most of my time back here in kitchens."

Ryan gave her a pointed look. "And you guys have been doing really well, despite operating in a town resistant to change or foreign ideas."

"What? Someone got offended by our French cooking? We cover all kinds of cuisines. Most American cuisine is technically foreign." She tried not to guffaw and failed.

"I'm not saying that they're against you ideologically, more like someone who doesn't want your businesses to succeed, for whatever reason. One way of looking at it is that you guys have only been in business for a few months, and you already had clients scheduling their events around your availability. Somebody was getting that work before you came along or was hoping to get it in the future."

"You're right, after we came along, all of Houston's fine-dining caterers lost their corner of the Seagrass upscale market. I bet they're real protective of a territory that requires them to drive an hour and a half there and back with refrigerated trucks." Ashley was still having trouble taking the idea seriously.

"You guys really have no other competition

in town?"

"Well, if you're talking about them competing on our level, not even close." she replied, flipping her hair haughtily for emphasis, if not comic relief. Ryan threw a sour cream and onion chip at her. "But seriously, the options for catering in Seagrass are barbecue, Mexican food, barbecue, seafood, barbecue, barbecue...and the seafood guys mostly do fried stuff and 'bring your own catch.' Not many upscale events want to make guests catch their own food next to a smelly gutting station."

"Just an idea." He shrugged. "You know, if it turns out that someone poisoned your cream puffs, it might be worth putting in surveillance cameras at Fresh Start Kitchens. If someone is trying to blame Seagrass Sweets for Colleen's murder, they might try messing with your food again to make it look like a pattern of negligence."

"You say that like there's another reason someone might want us to go out of business."

Ashley responded, when something on her monitor caught her eye. "Hey, wait. Remember me saying that I'll know it when I see it?"

She motioned him over and began rewinding the footage. It was a little dark at that point, but they could clearly see a tall, heavyset man with a familiar bald spot.

"We're looking at it."

Ryan was squinting at the screen. "Is that Smoke Daddy Lee?"

Ashley nodded, taking note of the time stamp. "Yup. Going in the service entrance, even though he's not cooking. This is around the time that I must have left to rearrange the desserts, meaning that he was out of my sight by the time I got back. Why would he be in such a hurry to go in and out?"

She pulled up time-synced side-by-side footage of the parking lot and the side door where they saw Colleen coming in, fast forwarding to the estimated time Ashley remembered her arriving.

"Huh?" Ryan said. "I don't remember seeing him as a guest. He's not dressed for it, either."

"He wouldn't dress appropriately for his own wedding," Ashley commented, shaking her head.

A small, red sedan was seen pulling into the parking lot, and the disheveled Colleen power-walked inside, glancing behind her along the way. Not long after, a blue pickup parked on the opposite side, close to the service door, and out stepped the last person Ashley had hoped to see. And here she thought that Hope had been jumping to conclusions blaming him.

"No way." Ryan blurted. "They arrived not even a minute apart. Either that's a huge coincidence, or—"

Ashley sighed. "Or Colleen was being followed by Smoke Daddy Lee."

CHAPTER 11

UNABLE TO SLEEP, Ashley got up before sunrise and started baking. The dark of early morning was occupied by bakers all over the world, creating something fresh before the rest of the world woke to eat. In Paris, when she was studying to bake under Patty, she loved finishing up the last batch of the day's bread and then sitting next to the window, watching café owners wake up the street. They'd arrive at their cafés, roll up the gates, bring out the tables, sweep the bricks under the tables and start the espresso machines. Ashley had big dreams for Seagrass Sweets; it might be only catering now, but she hoped to open her own patisserie one day. When she did, these early mornings—when the day was still topped with the dew of possibility—would be her routine, not just the occasional delight.

She decided to make fresh fruit tartlets to bring over to the McCays, whom she was planning to visit this evening. The murder was frustrating her; the lack of a clear path to follow had kept her up all night. The way she saw it, she had three suspects with motive: Emma Phee, who was having an affair with Bobby that Colleen knew about; Smoke Daddy Lee, a Localist who had followed Colleen into the banquet and was upset about her encouraging Bobby to sell to a hotel developer and Monty Gahn, the fracker who may have been taking advantage of Bobby's illness to negotiate a land sale.

Then there was Eddie. Eddie, who had basically thrown a grenade into Ashley's original path and sent her back to square one. Eddie, who claimed he was having an affair with Colleen which she was scheming to protect by double-crossing Bobby. The details of Eddie's story fit what Ashley heard in the bathroom, but there was still something that didn't sit right; she couldn't put her finger on it, but there was something suspicious about him. She hoped the surveillance she and Ryan were doing on him—his webcam and the keylogger—as well as the data she might soon find on the flash drive would help her pinpoint exactly what didn't fit.

She mulled over the details of the case as she delicately placed pieces of fruit in a symmetrical pattern on the tiny little tartlets. Two blueberries, a kiwi slice, a strawberry, a peach slice and a tiny leaf of lemon basil fit snugly atop the creamy filling. It was meditative work that helped her clear her mind.

Driving up the long driveway of the McCays' house, Ashley admired the yellow blooms that gave no hint of the decline happening inside the impressive house. Bobby may not be long for this world, but the Hinckley's columbines lining the driveway were a sunshine yellow that brought to mind nothing but eternal summer. It may have been morbid for her to prioritize speaking with Bobby before seeking out Emma on account of his limited time left, but she needed to get answers quickly. Besides, she knew that Emma wasn't leaving town in a hurry, for the same reason. She could almost feel Emma circling Bobby and his estate like a starving vulture.

While she waited for Bobby, Ashley wandered around the garden, admiring his roses, rare flowers and plants, each meticulously labeled with a nameplate stuck at its base. She felt drawn to the elegant and delicate Lagerfeld roses. As she buried her nose in them, inhaling deeply, she was transported back to her birthday years ago, in the basement office where she worked with Ryan. They had walked into the office from a celebratory lunch and found a dozen of the pale pink roses on her desk. At first, she didn't know who they were from. Sliding her finger underneath the sealed envelope, she kept looking at Ryan and had the strangest feeling in her chest, like a balloon expanding with each breath. When she read the card and saw that they were from Sergey, whom she hadn't heard from in weeks, the balloon popped, leaving her feeling inexplicably grumpy the rest of the day.

Her memories were interrupted by a shrill voice coming from the patio. It was Bobby's nurse, Georgie, a matronly no-nonsense, middle-aged woman who seemed older than her years. She was setting the brakes on Bobby's wheelchair.

"Mr. McCay will see you now," she said. Then she came closer to Ashley so that Bobby couldn't hear. "But only for a short while; he gets tired easily and leaves us from time to time."

Ashley smiled and rushed up the steps towards him, momentarily horrifying the nurse.

As she approached the old man, she was struck by just how much he had deteriorated since the last time she saw him. She did her best not to show it on her face.

"Hello, Mr. McCay." She reached out and gingerly took his hands.

He smiled weakly and chided, "Bobby, dear girl, don't make me feel older than I already am."

They laughed as Georgie slowly turned on her heel and made her way back into the house, stopping here and there to throw a cautionary glance over her crisp, white shoulder.

"Are you sure it's okay to talk out here?" Ashley asked, crossing her arms and rubbing the slight chill off her shoulders.

"Oh, yes, I love the sweet perfume from my flowers on the night air. Don't worry about me."

He took in a deep sniff and smiled with his eyes closed in rapture, then opened them slowly. "Would you like some iced tea or lemonade?"

"No, thanks. How are you these days, or is that a stupid question?"

"Oh, no, but I mustn't complain. Who would listen anyway?"

His smile slowly dissolved into a look of confusion. Glancing at her face, he seemed to be suddenly unaware of who she was.

"I'm sure there are many people who'd listen, and I'm the least of them."

As they caught each other up on their family members and shared acquaintances, Bobby's answers were short and his eyes dull. But as soon as she mentioned his business, a spark seemed to light up his eyes, flickering brightly one minute, then fading the next.

"After all my years in business, my greatest satisfaction these last few years was selling bait and tackle. I know it sounds clichéd, but I enjoy the simple life, always have."

Ashley smiled warmly. "Retirement looks good on you," she lied.

His eyes glazed over as he looked out into

the distance. "Yeah, I will probably do one last deal, then hang up the hat for good."

She leaned forward and squeezed his upper arm tenderly. This jolted him back, giving them both a start, followed by chuckles.

"Ooh, don't scare me, girl. I don't need a heart attack on top of being sick."

Ashley apologized and made a mental note to keep her hands to herself. Bobby pulled himself up in the wheelchair with a small grunt. She knew he was the kind of man who loved to talk about work. She hoped that by smiling and showing interest, she could get him talking without it seeming like she was snooping.

"Is the Bayview deal your last hurrah?" she asked.

He looked at her, surprised, and then sighed. "I suppose everyone knows by now. Yes, I have a gentleman's agreement to sell a parcel near the Mouth for a hotel; the paperwork is being drawn up. I hate thinking some oversized tourist trap may become my legacy, but I have to think about my wife. She made a lot of sacrifices for me over the years. I owe it to her to provide a comfortable life after I'm gone. In any case, at least it's just a hotel and not those frackers."

"Paperwork—boy, that's always stressful. What is that, like a geological survey?" She smiled and tilted her head, feeling so cheesy. But Bobby didn't seem to notice.

"Nah. Much simpler than that. I've done it a hundred times in my career; you go back and forth on an offer, have an assessor draw up a survey of the property lines, grit your teeth through the final negotiations and then sign in front of a lawyer. Nothing out of the ordinary."

"Is this deal with Monty Gahn? I keep hearing his name around town."

"Lord, no." he exclaimed. "That man is just a sore loser. When he discovered he lost the property to Bayview, he went back to Houston with his tail between his legs. I'm proud to be the one who ran that lowlife out of town."

"Now if only you could get the Localists to do the same."

"Yeah, they've been causing me some trouble these last few weeks. They set fire to a shed of mine a few weeks back. I'd wish they'd stick to smoking meat instead of other people's property."

So Bobby didn't order the geological survey. Then who did? Also, if Gahn was seen arguing with Colleen the night of her murder and then skipped town, that was one heck of a coincidence. And Bobby seemed to be implying that Smoke Daddy Lee, Seagrass's resident meat smoker, was involved.

Bobby coughed a few times, which prompted the nosy nurse to step out of the shadows, giving Ashley a stern look before retreating. It was all Ashley could do to keep from poking her tongue out. She was still—at heart—a precocious teenager.

"Do you have any idea who these Localists are? I think they might have something to do

173

with Colleen's death."

He gave her a vague stare and began fidgeting around with the blanket on his knee. She reached out her hand but stopped; she didn't want to give him a heart attack.

"Bobby?" she asked softly.

He snapped out of it and shook his head, which slowly turned into a nod as he smiled at her affectionately. "I've always looked at you as a daughter, Ashley. You've always been a great friend to Hope. We all appreciate that."

A cloud of confusion passed over Bobby's face. In a panic, Ashley sensed that time was running out. She needed to know who the Localists were so she could figure out where they were the night of the murder. As she waited for his response, it became clear that it was already too late. The lurking nurse came back out and gently chided her charge while glaring at Ashley like she was the Grim Reaper.

"It's time for your medication, Mr. McCay."

He looked over at Georgie and gave her an

equally confused look, which soon dissipated. He seemed to be veering back and forth, in and out of it as time went on.

"Yes, I am rather tired." He rubbed his temples, fingers wavering ever so slightly.

Ashley felt bad for being so impetuous, but she had to try one last time before she left.

"I'm so sorry, Bobby, but I wanted to ask a few more questions. I want to ask you about Emma."

Bobby's head jerked towards her at the mention of Emma's name; his hesitant frown broke into a shining smile. He stared at the sky as twilight began to descend.

"It's glorious, you know. So glorious—out there—at night."

"Pardon?"

"The night, Hope. You know how lovely it is. You always loved this time of day, didn't you, Hope?"

"It's Ashley; I'm Ashley."

Her concern about not getting the information she needed was overtaken by the sadness she felt over this once-strapping business man devolving into a shell of his former self.

Georgie started to bristle. "I think he's had enough, haven't you, Mr. McCay?"

"Yes, Emma. You're right. I've had enough." He patted the hand Georgie had placed on his shoulder. "You treat me so kindly, Emma."

The nurse smiled apologetically at Ashley. "I'm sorry, but it's getting worse. He has his good days and his bad days. One moment he's totally lucid and the next? Well, you saw for yourself."

Ashley nodded and started making her way across the garden. On her way to her car, she felt her phone vibrating in her jacket pocket. Once she answered, she was almost sorry that she had.

"Hey, girly—it's Mueller—and you won't guess what I found out."

Ashley had had enough confusion for one

evening. Even though she wasn't in the mood for games, she tried not to be rude while asking him to speak plainly for once.

"I don't want to guess, just tell me."

"The poison. Guess."

He seemed like an excited child. She could hear him panting and wondered if he was under a bush or at his desk.

"Just tell me, won't you?"

"Alrighty, then. Wait for it... It comes from an exotic flower."

"What kind of exotic flower? Do you know?" She was blurting loudly in her excitement. She grew more impatient when he started to stammer as he attempted to pronounce the name.

"Wait a minute, girly, I'm reading it off the toxicology report right here. Solansy—it's a solankey—related to datturra or something. I think it's tryin' to say brugmansion. Boy, this thing ought to have a pronunciation guide or something." He stuttered a few more times while Ashley turned around and headed toward

177

the McCays' garden.

"Could you just spell it for me?"

"Alrighty. It's B.r.u.g.m.a.n.s.i.a. Got it?"

"I've never heard of that," Ashley said, crouching to read the labels on the pots near her feet. She didn't know why she thought she'd find it here, but she had a hunch.

"Trumpet flower is the common name."

Just then, she felt her spine tingling as she laid eyes on a small, potted tree with delicate, peach-colored trumpet flowers cascading from its branches. She walked over and bent down to read the pot's label, staked into the soil. Sure enough, it read "Brugmansia: from the family Solanaceae."

She stood up and filled her lungs with the cool night air, wondering who else had access to these gardens. A vision of Emma Phee walking through them with Bobby popped to mind, the same image that had been captured in a photograph and was on Colleen's phone.

CHAPTER 12

ASHLEY AWOKE EARLY the next morning and wanted to call Ryan right away to share the news about the poison. When she checked her phone, though, she saw that he still hadn't answered her text from the previous night, so she decided to distract herself with baking. She didn't want to be *that* girl, the one who texted to ask why he hadn't texted. She and Ryan were finally close to a friendship without awkwardness, like they had so many years ago, and she didn't want to ruin it by being overeager. More than ever, she understood the need for personal time and space in a friendship, and she was willing to foster it in theirs, no matter how difficult it was.

The aroma of the lemon she was zesting for her lemon poppy seed muffins woke her up, filling her with optimism for the day. Just as she opened the oven door to put the muffins in, she heard her phone buzz. It was a text from Ryan saying she should come over whenever she could; he was still at home, so she could meet him there.

When he opened the door to his apartment, Ashley leaned in to give him a hug, but she was holding the basket of muffins on her hip, so at the last minute, she offered her left hand for a high-five. It threw both of them off balance and sent the basket cascading to the floor. To make things even more awkward, Dizzy pounced on the muffins and licked half the basket's worth before Ashley could shove her away.

"This is why you always double your recipe, right?" Laughing, Ryan stood up to hold the door open.

Dizzy raced up to him, lemon filling and

sweet, white meringue stuck in her whiskers.

"Dizzy, no." Ashley commanded.

It was too late. She'd jumped up and spread half of the mess all over Ryan's jeans. Luckily, he wasn't fazed. He laughed harder and playfully wrestled Dizzy to the ground, where she immediately rolled over and lapped up the attention.

"That dog will be the death of me." Ashley snapped half-heartedly, but she smiled when Ryan reached out for the basket and grabbed her elbow to pull her into the apartment.

They sat on his couch with the muffins, fresh coffee and his laptop open to the Wikipedia page on Brugmansia.

"Trumpet flowers, related to Datura." Ashley read, scrolling down the screen.

"They're quite stunning," said Ryan.

"And deadly. They're poisonous, and that's what they found in the contents of Colleen's stomach."

"Speaking of stomachs, mine is happy.

These muffins are delicious. You never disappoint."

She smiled but then made a face at Dizzy, who was still licking the debris off her face and paws.

"So," Ryan said through a mouthful of muffin, "we know about the poison, even though it's assumed that you didn't put it there."

"Oh, shut up." She gave him a little shoulder-to-shoulder shove.

"I imagine that you'd like to watch some surveillance video? I found something interesting from that newly installed camera in the commercial kitchen."

"Yes, but I have more information first. I met with Bobby McCay. It was sad; he's really deteriorating physically, and mentally too, I fear. "

She told him about how Bobby admitted to making a gentleman's agreement to sell the Mouth to hotel developers, which sent Monty Gahn back to Houston.

"The strange thing, though, is that he said

there was no geological survey for shale gas deposits involved in the deal. He also implied the Smoke Daddy Lee was behind the vandalism attributed to the Localists. Then he really started making no sense and confused his nurse with Emma, and it got too sad for me to stay. Who knows if anything he said is even true? The whole visit may have been a waste; it didn't turn up any new leads."

"It's all evidence, even if it is all fantasies of his dementia. Plus, you found the trumpet flower in the McCays' garden. It could be the source of the poison. Let's not throw the baby out with the bathwater, Watson."

Ashley wasn't in the mood to kid around, but she appreciated Ryan trying to cheer her up. "Firstly, let's get one thing straight, you're Watson and I'm Holmes. Secondly, I've been thinking about those photos of Emma Phee and Bobby at his residence. If that trumpet flower is indeed the murder weapon, she certainly had access to it. I'm sure they took a few romantic midnight strolls in the garden."

"Oh, that reminds me, I have some video footage I want to show you from Fresh Start Kitchens. Nothing too out of the ordinary has happened since you installed the cameras, except this." He brought up the video on his computer.

On the screen, Smoke Daddy Lee and Patty were talking in the kitchen. She was leaning back against the counter with one hand behind her back and the other twirling a wispy strand of blonde hair, her head slightly tilted to one side. Smoke Daddy Lee was standing a few feet away, telling a story that they could not hear over the muted video feed, but it was obviously funny by the way Patty laughed animatedly every few minutes, covering her mouth with her hand and bending over slightly. Lee was moving closer to Patty, step by step, as he told the story. The more she laughed, the closer he came to her, and the more they both smiled. The video was playing at 3x real-time, and the speed made Patty and Lee's gestures more pronounced, like an old slapstick comedy film.

"Are they flirting?" Ashley was quite shocked to see Patty with anything but a professional demeanor.

"It looks that way. Keep watching."

Lee was now standing right in front of Patty and his demeanor had changed. The storytelling comedian was gone and a bashful schoolboy stood in his place, nervously wringing his hands. Patty was watching him intently until they both stopped talking. Patty then broke the tension by grabbing a tea towel and playfully slapping him with it, making them both laugh.

"Oh, Lord." Ashley groaned. "Thank goodness for mute."

"Actually, you are going to want to hear this part," said Ryan, turning up the volume.

"Oh, go on." Patty beamed at Lee, apparently enjoying herself immensely.

"Ya don't think this ol' boy is serious? I

didn't want to say anything in front-a lil' Ashley, but I came down to the banquet that night hopin' to ask you out. I lost mah nerve and ended up leavin', little lady."

"Really? I don't even know what you're talking about."

"Surely you do, a world-weary gal like yusself."

She giggled again, while closing in to tap him on the chest gently with her wooden spoon.

Lee laughed loudly, obviously enjoying her flirting.

"Please, turn it off." Ashley was squirming in her seat. "It feels so wrong to be spying on my friends like this."

"I agree, but it did show us that Lee had other things in mind when he came to the banquet that night," said Ryan.

"Well, now I feel bad for spying on my friend *and* for suspecting an innocent man for murder. I'm going to have to get rid of that hidden camera right away."

186

He stopped the video. "Yeah. For all the sleuthing and spying you've done, you still have a great heart, Ash."

She shrugged. "I've seen people hurt those they love and hope to get away with it; I never want to let myself get even close to that." She felt him looking at her, his face just a foot away from hers, but she couldn't turn to face him.

"Anyway," she continued, "I guess Lee is out as a suspect. And if what Bobby said is true, Gahn looks mores suspicious than ever, but we'd have to go to Houston to get hold of him. That leaves Emma. And Eddie. I know he's your friend, but his story doesn't add up. There's something nagging at me about it. Still, I can't understand why he would want to kill Colleen."

Ryan had gobbled down another handful of muffin. He was doing his best to chew and swallow so he could respond, while licking his fingers and sweeping crumbs off himself and the table.

187

"Well, I might have a hunch." He pulled a keylogger report up on his laptop and pointed to it with a lemon meringue fingertip. He quickly stuffed his finger in his mouth to lick it before continuing.

"Now, stay with me on this. Eddie has been Googling things like 'honeymoon destinations' and silly lists such as 'romantic gifts for your wife.' However, when I checked into the thumb-drive you stole from Eddie—"

Ashley shook her finger at him. "I'm not a thief. I like to think of it as borrowing."

"OK. When I checked the thumb drive which you 'appropriated' from Eddie, I found this." He waved his hand triumphantly.

She leaned forward to squint at the screen. "Wedding plans, honeymoon options, a budget...Oh!" Ashley glanced at Ryan, her eyebrows raised. "This is interesting. 'Note to self—how much can the McCays pay?' Well, well, well."

She leaned back, jumping when Dizzy—who

was trying to insinuate herself between the two of them on the couch—let out a sharp bark.

"Dizzy, get down."

Instead of obeying, Dizzy scooted her hind-legs behind Ryan's back, stretched her front paws behind Ashley and finally rested her head against the couch's back cushion.

"Look here, you missed something." Ryan pointed to the screen again. "His bank statements, personal and business. He's broke."

She took a closer look and nodded slowly. "Wow, he's in bad shape."

"Both himself and the business."

"Okay," Ashley mused. "He wanted to marry Hope because the family's money would help him and his business considerably."

Ryan nodded. "Maybe he killed Colleen to keep the affair in the dark because she was getting so close to revealing it."

"Right, because that would ensure his marriage to Hope. But how can we prove that?" She leaned back again and Dizzy yelped in protest, although she didn't move.

"I don't know. Plus, Hope knew about the affair, and she was going to take him back. It doesn't add up."

Ashley rubbed her eyes in frustration. She stood up and took the basket of muffins to the kitchen, where she refilled her mug with fresh coffee.

"Well, we still have to find out what Emma was fishing around for in Colleen's purse, but it seems that Eddie is suspect number one until proven otherwise," Ryan said.

Ashley went back to the couch and sat down in a huff, prompting Dizzy to whine quietly and readjust her position.

"I don't like talking to Emma. It's been years since high school, but when I talk to her, I feel like that dorky computer nerd watching the cheerleaders practice their dance moves at lunch while I write code on my laptop."

"Awww, come on, Ash. We all know the nerds end up way cooler than the cheerleaders later in life, when it really matters." He put his arm around her, giving her shoulder a little squeeze.

"It's okay, I'll talk to her–for Colleen's sake."

"And for the sake of Seagrass Sweets and The Southern Bird, remember?" He rose from the couch and took his coffee cup into the kitchen.

Ashley sighed and stood up as well. She looked a Ryan's clock and was so shocked to see how much time had passed, she double-checked her phone. The time had flown by and, though inertia and the comfort of Ryan's couch begged her to stay, she called for Dizzy and made her way to the door.

"Thanks for your help," she said. "It means a lot to me that you're helping me out."

From the kitchen and out of her sight, Ryan responded, "Are you kidding me? It's just like old times. I haven't had this much fun in, well..." He appeared in the kitchen doorway, wiping his hands on a towel and smiling. "Let's just say that I was such a dork back in high school that I never even ate lunch in the cafeteria; it was too risky on account of all the jocks looking for guys like me to pick on so they could look tough. I'm having a lot of fun hanging out with you again, Ash."

She smiled back, while Dizzy pawed at the door. "We nerds need to stick together." They stood and looked at each other for a long moment, then she turned and let Dizzy scramble to the car.

CHAPTER 13

ASHLEY LOVED HER early morning walks with Dizzy before most of the world had gotten out of bed. They would walk to a dog park near her house and usually have the place to themselves. On this particular morning, the air was cool enough that she was happy to run around with Dizzy, chasing the dog around until she found herself a bit winded. She sat on a picnic bench in the shade under large trees and watched Dizzy sniff around, chasing bunnies and shadows, not sure if she could actually distinguish the two. The morning's quiet calmed her and gave her a clear head. While Dizzy darted around and sniffed everything in sight, Ashley thought about her friendship with Ryan.

When they first met, he had a long-distance girlfriend. This gave them a lot of time to hang out together outside of work, doing things that would be considered dates, even though their relationship could only be platonic. By the time Ryan and his girlfriend realized neither or them was willing to move and decided to call it quits, Ashley had started seeing Serge. While she still saw Ryan every day at work, their time together did not extend beyond that as Serge swept her off her feet in a spell of romance and intrigue funded by a seemingly endless source of affluence.

Of course, after she moved to Paris with Serge, she realized that all of it—the romance, the love, the money—was an illusion. Yes, she missed Ryan when she moved to Paris, but if she was honest with herself, she already missed him in Seagrass when she was busy dating Serge. Now, back in Seagrass after all the madness Serge had created, the one thing that seemed unequivocally positive was the chance to spend time with Ryan again. So why wasn't she happy? Why did it feel like her friendship with Ryan wasn't enough?

She called Dizzy over and put her leash back on so they could walk home. Ashley wanted to get to Fresh Start Kitchens early enough to finish all the prep for their event that afternoon. A few minutes after they left the dog park, she was nearly bowled over by Emma Phee, who had come around suddenly from a bend while jogging along the same path.

"Oh, sorry." Ashley said to the flustered woman, who was jogging with full makeup already in place. Emma pulled the white earbuds out of her ears and continued to jog in place.

"For God's sake, Ashley. You certainly do have a habit of getting in the way."

"I'm sorry. Geez, you run a lot." Ashley snapped, which wasn't how she usually addressed Ms. Emma Phee and her ilk.

Emma put her hands on her hips and cocked her head, seemingly concerned all of a sudden, before lifting her arms in a jumping jack motion. "What's got you in a flap?"

195

Ashley decided that the time was ripe for some unabashed questioning, secretly marveling at the fact that she had been afforded the opportunity to speak with Emma so soon.

"Oh, I guess my head is in a swirl with the investigation and all. It's horrible to think that we have a murderer in our midst, wouldn't you agree?"

Watching closely for Emma's response, Ashley wasn't surprised when she stopped jogging and stared like she'd just been slapped in the face. Dizzy had circled back, trying to jump up on Emma, but she wouldn't have it. She turned away like a child, with her arms up around her face.

"Please, get your mutt away from me."

"She's not a mutt. She's a good, faithful dog." Ashley defended her like a mother protecting her child against a monster.

Emma balked. "Oh, I suppose that jibe was directed at me and my history with men, right?"

Ashley was shocked. She hadn't meant it in

any such way, but suddenly, she saw an opportunity.

"I'm sorry. I didn't mean it that way, but since we're on the subject—"

"Oh, please, spare me."

Emma wiped nonexistent sweat away from her flawless pink face with her flawless pink wristbands. Her outfit was so outrageously stylish and coordinated, it made Ashley want to squirt beetroot juice all over it. She wasn't usually mean, but Emma seemed to bring out the worst in her.

She decided to go for broke. "Well, I spoke with Sheriff Mueller, and he told me something quite interesting."

"Really? Was it about Colleen's purse?" Emma eyed Ashley like she had made a winning jab in a jousting tournament.

This startled Ashley, as she wasn't expecting such an early admission. "Um, yes, actually."

"And you're wondering what I was looking

for." Emma smirked, looking smug.

"I guess so. Yeah," Ashley replied, still not believing her luck.

The women stared at each other like they were in the middle of a mental chess match, eyebrows tilted, waiting for the other to crack. Ashley half expected to look around and see that time had stood still. Seeing as Emma was—for the moment—tight-lipped, Ashley put the cherry on top, as it were.

"Also, just so you know, I had a wonderful meeting with Bobby McCay the other night, even though he's a little worse for wear, with his illness and all that."

She watched Emma's face carefully for any sign of a crack appearing in her perfect visage. It didn't take long for Emma to start dissolving, slowly but surely, while still managing to keep her immaculate façade in-check.

"Girl, you are nosy. If you must know, yes, I was having an affair with Bobby; okay? Satis-fied? Now, I imagine I fit the bill. Typical gold-digger, right?"

Ashley wasn't expecting such a big confession so quickly, but she maintained her composure.

"Okay." She wanted to kick herself for such a lame comeback, as if she needed one.

"I was looking for any evidence I could find about the affair," Emma continued.

Ashley frowned. "What evidence could've been in Colleen's purse?"

Emma sighed, over-exaggerating her annoyance, slumping her shoulders dramatically and slamming her hands on her hips for emphasis. "Colleen was trying to blackmail me. She knew about the affair and was following us. She was taking pictures and everything, that little snoop. In a town this small, I wouldn't have survived a week if people found out, so I had to make sure I destroyed any pictures she may still have had. Bobby and I were in love, but who would see it that way?"

Now Emma was breaking down, fighting angry tears and holding her hands over her heart like she was going for an Oscar. Ashley stood silently while her mind raced to rearrange the pieces of the puzzle. Her silence only served to encourage Emma to spill more beans, such as they were. Now her voice was starting to sound whiny, making her façade slip further and further as her woeful act reached its peak.

"It wasn't hard for Colleen to figure out where we were meeting, since she knew Bobby's schedule. And you know what? I'll admit it, I was glad when she was found dead, but I did not murder her! I haven't the faintest idea who would've murdered her, and I can prove it."

Ashley narrowed her eyes in disbelief. "How?"

Emma gasped like the drama queen she was and wiped away a fake tear before continuing. Ashley had to suppress a laugh.

"Eddie asked me to leave the banquet early. Colleen must have told him about my affair with Bobby because he came at me cussing and angry, saying I'd better get out of there before I upset the McCay family. Honestly, Bobby's wife is a woman who is happy to focus on glittery gifts and turn a blind eye to her unscrupulous husband's pastimes, so long as the glitter keeps coming. She knows, but I didn't see the point in rubbing her face in it, so I left early."

Emma was telling the truth. Of course, it was obvious that she wanted to clear her name, but to reveal that much about her personal life would've been torture for the glamorous and supposedly sophisticated socialite.

"Wow, Emma. I don't know what to say."

"It doesn't much matter anymore. Our affair ended a while ago on account of Bobby losing his mind. He stopped recognizing me when I'd visit. His wife can have him now, for all I care."

"Okay—well—I'm sorry, Emma. This has been tough on all of us, I guess."

"Don't be. What Bobby and I had was special, but nothing lasts forever, right?" Emma was slowly picking up the pace of her jogging in place. "Well, am I off the hook?" Before Ashley could respond, she put her earbuds back in and jogged away.

Dizzy chased her for a few paces. "Get your mutt off me. Shoo!" Emma called back, trying to kick her before taking off down the path.

Dizzy trotted back to her mistress, proud as punch. Ashley didn't bother to answer Emma's question about being off the hook. She stood and watched her jogging away, feeling like she was also watching the case disappearing into the horizon.

By the time she made it to Fresh Start Kitchens, she felt spent. She had been so energized by the early morning, but the case was now completely occupying her thoughts. After talking to Emma, Ashley was convinced that Eddie was the murderer. She just had to figure out how to prove it.

As Ashley walked in the kitchens, Patty was chopping cilantro. When she looked up and saw her business partner in an obvious state, she left the stove and walked over.

"Hey, partner." she called out, trying to inject some light into Ashley's subdued aura. "Penny for your thoughts?"

"Hey." Ashley was embarrassed by this kind of attention; normally, Patty would say hello but not abandon her work. Mustering her best smile, she tried to wave it off like nothing was wrong.

"I am not taking no for an answer," Patty stated.

"If you say so." Still smiling, Ashley put out her hand for the penny.

"Okay. Now fill me in."

"It's the case. I don't know if I'll ever figure out what happened to Colleen. I saw Emma Phee, and she isn't the murderer, so I'm at a dead end." She neglected to mention that Smoke Daddy Lee was still on her suspect list.

Patty looked at Ashley, really looked at her. "So, it's the case that has you looking so glum?

Just the case, huh?" She raised an eyebrow and the right corner of her tight smile.

She thought about trying to tell Patty about her feelings for Ryan, but when she tried to think of what to say, she didn't even know. She was confused about why she was bothered, which bothered her even more.

"I guess. For now, it's just the case." She gave her partner a look that she hoped said, *please, ask me again later.*

"All right, then," said Patty "let's get to work to take your mind off the case. Some people have great insights into unanswered questions while in the shower; I usually have them in the kitchen." She turned back to the stove and continued stirring the vegetable stock she was making for the base of the soupe à l'oignon on the day's menu.

As Ashley kneaded and turned yeasted dough for the croissants, her mind quieted and her thoughts slowed. She was completely focused on the task at hand, and before she knew it, she was feeling much better.

By the time they arrived at the luncheon, she was back to her old self. The Seagrass Elderly Citizen's Club was celebrating a recent win for one of their members, Lydia Fairmont, who was an avid chess player and a staunch alcoholic at the ripe old age of seventy-two. Nonetheless, she had won first prize in a small tournament, which had been held in England. Despite her drinking issues and bawdy behavior, she was always welcome wherever she went. Everyone loved her infectious sense of humor.

Seeing Ashley arrive, Maude came up and asked her if she was okay being back in the Gulf Coast Women's Club again. Ashley pretended it wasn't even an issue, advising that she was lucky to still be in operation. She omitted the fact that she had sat in her idling catering van in the parking lot for a five full minutes, working up the courage to come back to the scene of the crime.

The cucumber and cilantro pumpernickel sandwiches were a huge hit, along with Patty's soup. While the others helped plate Patty's famous cold, cilantro chicken and shredded beetroot with chili peppers and green onions, Ashley applied the finishing touches on her gorgeous petit fours. They included red velvet with cream cheese ganache, hazelnut shells and Kahlua wafers.

Sabine looked over her shoulder and whistled. "I sure hope we have enough champagne back here; these ladies are not joking around."

Ashley grinned. "Why not? You only live once."

"I'm amazed the old bird they're celebrating has lived as long as she has. Apparently she has quite a reputation for being a flirt." Patty added with a cheeky smirk.

"Then we're lucky Mark's off today. We don't want another scandal." Sabine giggled.

"What does that mean?" Ashley snapped, shocking the others.

Sabine blushed and looked to the others for support, but they averted their eyes. She was on her own for this one. "Sorry, Ashley, just kidding. I mean, that was thoughtless."

Ashley knew that she'd overreacted, but it was still a sore point and she was tired.

"It's okay. I guess I am a little on edge being back here. But don't even joke about scandals. We're still clawing our way back."

Sabine capitulated. "Of course. Sorry, Ashley. Really."

Ashley smiled. She couldn't stay mad at Sabine, with her youthful exuberance and loyal adoration for Seagrass Sweets.

"Aw, it's okay. Forgive me for snapping?" She reached out and tousled the girl's punky hair.

"Sure." Sabine smiled like a child who had escaped from a sticky situation.

They had a quick hug before Maude interrupted, gruff and impatient as usual.

"So, do they know what happened at the

banquet, hon?"

Ashley shrugged. "They're narrowing it down, but still guessing."

She didn't want to give too much away, knowing what a gossip Maude was.

"Forgive me for sayin' so, but I'll bet my last dollar it was that nasty Emma Phee." Sabine said.

"She has an alibi. It wasn't her." Patty advised as she dressed yet another salad.

Maude snorted. "Probably that ol' Smoke Daddy Lee."

Now it was Patty's turn to snap. "Of course it wasn't, Maude." Patty took a deep breath and smoothed the front of her apron with both hands. "I mean, he checks out. Right, Ashley?"

"Yes, he does. The police have their eye on another suspect."

She bit her lip for saying that much. She didn't want to be led into a discussion about the case, but she knew that she had to try and put a lid on it, for the sake of keeping the gossip in check.

"Who, then?" Maude asked.

"Never you mind who." Patty snapped again. "Like Ashley said, the police have it under control."

"Yes—but—you've been doing your own investigations, haven't you, Miss Ashley?" Sabine asked innocently.

Ashley picked up one of her trays and carefully carried it over to the dessert cart. "Of sorts, I guess. It wouldn't be right to leave it all up to those knuckleheads at the precinct."

The women laughed as Ashley checked her phone.

"Any time to chat today? About case?" she texted Ryan.

"*Something new?*" he texted back immediately.

"Emma Phee is out, leaving me back at square one. I'm thinking about going to see Eddie again."

She could see from the texting app that he

was writing his response right away.

"Alone? Could be unsafe. I'll come with you." Ashley was touched by his protectiveness, but she knew it would seem more casual and less of an attack if she went on her own. His reaction had made her feel special, even if only for a moment.

"Ur sweet, but I'll be fine. I'll call you after." She stared at her phone for a few minutes, hoping for a response. When none came, she turned it off and put it in her pocket.

"I'm off to run a quick errand. I'll meet you guys back at the kitchen, if that's okay." Patty nodded, waving her off. Ashley was so thankful to have Patty as a partner; they had an unspoken give and take approach to their work together. Someday, Patty would need to leave early, and without asking her why, Ashley would be happy to clean up on her behalf.

When she arrived at Eddie's trailer, he wasn't there. She looked through the windows to peer inside, but nothing seemed out of the ordinary. Driving back to the luncheon, she tried to piece together the case against Eddie. He had opportunity: he had been at the banquet and could easily have poisoned Colleen's food. Given the poison came from a flower that was grown on his future in-laws' property, access to it would be easy. He also had motive: wanting to keep his affair a secret so he could marry into the McCay family's money while Colleen was scheming up ways for them to betray Bobby and run off together. She needed proof, though. Sheriff Mueller would never be able to make a case based on all this speculation.

Her phone rang just as she parked her catering van outside Fresh Start Kitchens.

"Hey, are you still with Eddie?" It was Ryan on the other end.

She nearly giggled at his whispering, like it was all cloak and dagger.

"No, he's not home. We'll have to try again tomorrow."

"Phew," said Ryan. "I found something that

I can't figure out. I'll show you tomorrow. I guess the kayak trip will give us a chance to recharge our batteries. Then we can attack the case with a fresh approach."

Ashley hung her head in exhaustion. She'd forgotten about the trip. They had planned it before Colleen had died. All she wanted to do was to go home and collapse into bed for at least 48 hours. She groaned in protest but tried not to sound whiny.

"I really don't feel like it, Ryan. I don't know if I have the energy for the water."

"Oh. Alright then." He sounded deflated; his disappointment was palpable, which made her feel guilty.

"I'm sorry."

"Well, maybe a trip is just what you need. I say, let's do it. The weather's going to be great and you love a good kayak session, right? Once we get out there, you'll probably be so happy you did."

His level of enthusiasm was contagious. She

knew that he was right, and it didn't take long for her to feel the same level of excitement.

"Okay." The idea of a fun day became more and more appealing. "Let's do it, then."

"Alright."

They made arrangements, and Ashley texted Michael to remind him. He had his own kayak, but they would need to rent theirs from Bobby's bait and tackle shop.

Back in Fresh Start Kitchens, she found Patty putting the last of their dishes away.

"The party was great, although the guest of honor never showed. Turns out that Ms. Fairmont had been up partying all night and was too ill to make it to her own celebratory brunch. That didn't stop the other ladies at the Elderly Citizen's club." Patty giggled at Ashley's surprised face.

"Can you imagine? That old bird was up all night, apparently with a younger man, half her age, no less." Patty raised her eyebrows.

"Well, at least someone is getting some romance. I'd be happy to be half as active when I'm her age."

"You never know, dear," said Patty. "Love usually comes around as soon as you stop looking for it."

CHAPTER 14

THE NEXT DAY was a Saturday, and Ryan had advised that he would pick Ashley and Dizzy up at 6 a.m. The sun was already shining brightly, and Michael, who was a veteran marshland hunter and fisherman, was going to meet them at the estuary. Ryan was full of enthusiasm and became even more excited when he saw that Ashley had packed a picnic basket that could have fed an army.

"Ooh, what you have got there, Ms. Ashley?" he said with a mock southern accent.

"Wait and find out." She opened the hatch in the back of the car and placed the basket under a blanket.

She had worked all last evening to prepare their feast. BBQ pork rolls with Havarti cheese and marinated olives, fried chicken with a honey and black pepper glaze, devilled eggs made with cream and shallots, celery stuffed with lemon and cayenne cream cheese, tomato and dill pickle salad, and the leftover petit fours—along with a couple of bottles of champagne—were packed Tetris-style in the oversized basket. "We need ice for the champagne."

"Oh, la de dah." Ryan teased. "Champagne. What's the occasion?"

"No occasion. Leftovers and just for fun."

She pinched his cheek playfully and reminded him that Michael would be meeting them.

"Okay—yes—I forgot." His demeanor changed slightly.

"Sorry. Should I have not invited him?" she asked, suddenly in a mild panic.

Ryan sighed, then grinned encouragingly. "No, no, he's great. Good idea, actually."

"Why?" For some reason, she felt her stomach lurch. Or was it her heart?

He laughed. "He can fish us out if we fall in

or we're too drunk to swim."

She knew that wouldn't happen. Ryan had never been a big drinker, and she had such a low tolerance that she didn't allow herself to have more than one drink. She didn't want to end up embarrassing herself. Besides, she needed to keep her wits about her, to focus on the case.

"What was it you wanted to tell me? Something about Eddie that you mentioned yesterday?" Ashley tried to sound casual, but she had been thinking about it all morning.

"Oh, yeah. Remember how Eddie said that Colleen had found the survey by snooping through his emails? Well, I was finally able to recover the original email the attachment was downloaded from."

"Let me guess. It wasn't Eddie's?"

"No. In fact, it was sent to Colleen by someone who set up a throw-away account to stay anonymous."

"Why would Eddie lie about that?"

217

"Beats me."

As they drove, Ashley flipped through the pictures she had taken in Eddie's trailer to see if she had missed anything. Nothing seemed noteworthy—paperwork piled high on the table, dirty dishes in the kitchen sink, clothes strewn across the bed. One top in particular stood out; it was shimmery and pink, not something she could imagine Eddie wearing. She zoomed in on the picture and realized that half of the clothes on the bed were women's clothes. There was even some jewelry on the bedside table. That was odd, given his and Hope's separation, but Hope might have left things there before his confession. There was nothing else that stood out and certainly no evidence of making or delivering poison. As they approached the estuary, Ashley decided to let the case go for the time being and enjoy their kayak excursion.

Michael was already slipping on his gear and prepping his kayak when Ryan pulled up behind Michael's car and let Dizzy out. She ran straight to Michael—her biggest fan—and nearly bowled him over with his exuberance.

"Dizzy!" Michael called out as the happy canine leapt up into his arms. For anyone else, this would've been a mean feat, but Michael was nearly 6'3" and built like a Russian bodybuilder. Dizzy was licking all over his face as they made much of each other.

"Oh, these are the only kisses I've had in ages."

"Ewww. Michael." Ashley chided.

Ryan laughed, siding with her brother. "You gotta get it where you can, right?"

Michael continued hugging and squeezing Dizzy, doing his best to keep hold of her without falling over. "Right."

Ashley decided to ignore them and went to check that the picnic basket was still stowed under the blanket before starting to don her gear behind the car. The men shook hands, and Michael helped lift the kayak off Ryan's car while Dizzy did her usual inspections of the bushes and the riverbanks. Ryan went up to Bobby's fish and tackle shop, which doubled as a kayak rental outfitter, and soon returned with a double kayak and greetings from Mr. McCay.

They eventually launched, with Dizzy in Michael's kayak while Ashley and Ryan sat together. The weeping willows and sun-dappled water lulled her into a state of bliss as they paddled up the estuary. She was almost in a trance, until she spied a couple of men on the side of the channel.

"What are they up to?" she asked, pointing in their direction.

He followed her gaze and shrugged. "Looks like a couple of surveyors."

"Really? That's the McCays' property. I wonder if they are surveying it for the Bayview deal. Maybe we should go speak to them?"

Before Ryan could answer, she texted Michael so as to avoid alerting the surveyors. She waited, shoulders hunched, for his response; she knew he hated to be bothered by text any time, much less while out in the beautiful tranquility of the water. Luckily, he only turned his head towards her and nodded. They paddled over to the water's edge and got out.

"You just can't leave it alone, can you?" Michael asked with a wry smile.

She grinned back as Dizzy took off to investigate. Suddenly, a man came out of nowhere with his hand outstretched. Ashley sized him up, then cautiously stuck out her hand to shake his.

"Good mornin', folks. How can I be of assistance?"

Shaking his head, Michael rolled his eyes and jerked his thumb back at Ashley. "My sister can't help herself. She has to know everything, don't you, Ash?"

She did her best not to poke her tongue out but went along with the ruse, trying to sound like a nosy tourist. "Hey, I'm just curious. What's going on?"

Ryan joined in to make it look like they were

concerned citizens. "Yeah, is it okay to be out on the water?"

The man laughed. He was wearing a cowboy hat, snakeskin boots and a bolo tie. "Of course, nothing going on here. We're just working on a survey of the marshland here. Nothing to be concerned about."

Then another, younger man appeared from behind him, looking nervously at the group. "Hello? What's going on here?" he asked.

"It's no problem. Just a few locals wanting to see what's going on," the first man replied, still smiling.

They both studied everyone's faces, like they were waiting for something to happen. Ashley could sense that something was going on, but she couldn't be sure.

"So, you're conducting the survey for the Bayview hotel development?" she asked, as innocently as she could.

The younger man stared blankly while the first man smiled, a little more anxious now.

"Well, yes, we're surveying the surface area of the property. Now, you three aren't part of that Localist coalition, are you?"

Both men stared at the group. Ashley couldn't tell if he was serious, but before she could answer, the older gentleman just started laughing. "Oh, I'm just giving y'all a hard time. No offense, but you three don't look like you could harm a fly." That made him laugh even harder, shaking loose his cowboy hat. When he took it off, she could see his name embroidered inside the brim.

"Monty Gahn!" she exclaimed. "Are you Monty Gahn?"

"Guilty as charged," he smiled, sticking out his hand to shake hers.

Suddenly, Michael became agitated, frantically looking from side to side. "Where did Dizzy go?" Ashley wanted to ask Monty Gahn a dozen questions, but she knew this area was dangerous, between the snakes, gators and changing tide. As soon as Michael started marching through the grasslands, she said a quick good-bye to Gahn and the other man and followed closely behind her brother. When she looked back at the men, she saw them whispering to each other before disappearing behind the bushes. Ryan soon followed Ashley and Michael, all three temporarily forgetting about the surveyors and calling out Dizzy's name in earnest.

"Dizzy?" She beckoned, trying not to sound angry, as Dizzy was sensitive to her temper. When she couldn't hear the dog, she became worried that she'd either been bitten by a snake or had fallen into a hole somewhere. It wasn't like her to disappear like that.

They continued zigzagging through the grass and bushes, calling for Dizzy and growing louder and more concerned as time went on. After about fifteen minutes, Michael stopped and held up his hand. "I think I hear her."

Then they all heard Dizzy's familiar, happy barking. They rushed over to where the estuary opened up to the ocean, finding Dizzy covered in mud and frolicking on the beach. She'd stumbled upon the evidence of a construction-related survey, but there were no other survey-ors in sight.

"Dizzy. You naughty dog!" Ashley admon-ished her and rushed over to greet her, then winced as she jumped up with her wet and muddy paws. "Lovely." she said, patting the happy dog on the head before looking around at the markings and flags.

Obviously full of excitement, Dizzy bounded over to the men.

"What is this?" Ryan asked, scratching his head as he looked around.

"Looks like another survey going on," Mi-chael answered, but he was paying more atten-tion to Dizzy, scratching behind her ears. "Good girl, Diz."

All three started wandering around to check out the scene, Dizzy weaving in and out around their legs. Ashley made sure that she stayed close, but she seemed to be happy with all of them there in her new playground.

Ashley heard rustling in the grass behind them. She felt the little hairs on the back of her neck bristle as she turned around and saw the outline of someone who seemed to be sneaking around and spying on them. Soon the men followed her gaze, watching the shadow getting closer.

Feeling brave with two men and a dog to protect her, she called out, "Who's there?"

As soon as she'd spoken, Dizzy started growling, then ran off with the hairy ridge raised on her back before Ashley could stop her. Within seconds, she'd flushed the shadow out of the grass. It was the younger man from the previous site, now a little embarrassed and afraid.

He came rushing out of the grass with his hands up, shaking and wide-eyed, making Michael and Ryan snigger uncontrollably.

"Okay, okay. Get your dog off me!"

Dizzy hadn't done any harm, but Ashley was glad that she was able to frighten him, just a little.

"Dizzy, it's all right. Heel."

That command had never worked before, but she was proud when the dog came back to her side and sat down obediently, still growling deep in her throat.

The man approached them slowly with his head hung in defeat. Ashley was already prepared to interrogate him.

"What are you doing? Why are you spying on us?"

"I wasn't really spying; well, I just had to make it look like I was spying," he replied in a wavering voice. "Mr. Gahn sent me over to see what you find. Listen, I can't afford to lose my job, so I've got to follow orders."

"Why would he send you to spy on us? He seemed friendly enough."

He gulped and looked at Ryan and Michael

before continuing. "He doesn't want you to figure out that there are two surveys going on here."

Ryan joined in the questioning, having overcome his schoolboy antics. "Why two surveys?"

The man looked down at his feet and then looked up, his face growing as red as beetroot. In the distance, they could hear Monty Gahn calling out for him to return.

"We were officially hired to do just one, but those of us on the crew with experience know that we are doing two—one for property lines and the other for shale deposits. I love Seagrass and want to protect it as much as anyone, but I have a family to feed, so I can't say anything that puts my job at risk. Everything I have to say, I already sent in the email." Gahn's voice was growing louder as he got closer.

"The email? Did you send an email to Colleen?"

"I've got to go; I can't say more." The man looked regretfully at the group, then scampered off and quickly disappeared into the grassland. Ashley disregarded his comment and called after him.

"Why Colleen? Why not Mr. McCay or his daughter?"

But the man was gone, leaving Ashley with her questions unanswered. She looked at Ryan and Michael, dumbfounded.

"Okay, well, that's that then." Michael exclaimed, breaking out in a huge, incredulous smile. "I don't know about you guys but I'm famished."

"Me too," Ryan said. "Let's get back and have ourselves a picnic."

He winked at Ashley and turned to follow Michael, followed in turn by Dizzy, barking her approval. Ashley made sure that she had a firm hold on Dizzy's collar as they continued back to the shore. Once they'd returned to the kayaks and pushed off, Ryan and Ashley talked about the night of the banquet, spurred on by the recent developments.

"You know what? I think I misinterpreted the implication of Colleen's statement."

"Which statement?" Ryan asked over his shoulder while he paddled.

"When she said, 'our future here in Seagrass.' I think Colleen was talking about the future of Seagrass—the environmental future of Seagrass, not her and Eddie's future together. She was such an environmentalist, I just can't believe that she would betray that for money. I think she was trying to protect Seagrass by threatening to reveal whatever that survey implied."

"Well, if she was talking only about Seagrass's future and not theirs, then maybe they weren't having an affair at all."

"Yeah, that's what I'm starting to think." Ashley's heart was starting to sink at the thought.

"Hmm." Ryan sounded like he was deep in thought.

She puzzled over it as they paddled back to

shore. The problem was, her stomach was competing with her brain for dominance. Thoughts of the delicious chicken and BBQ rolls took precedence, although she wondered what this new information could possibly mean.

Having arrived back where they started, they pulled their kayaks up on the beach and went to get the food from the car. Ashley laid out a couple of blankets on the edge of the estuary, while Ryan carefully placed the picnic basket in the center. As the men "oohed" and "aahed" over the food, she munched absent-mindedly, barely paying attention to their jokes and stories about whitewater rafting and other adventures.

When Michael popped the cork from one of the champagne bottles, Ashley nearly jumped out of her skin.

"Whoa, little lady." he laughed. "Where have you been?"

Dizzy happily fetched the cork from the bushes and brought it back to Ryan. He couldn't help but feed her yet another deviled egg as a reward.

"You'll regret that on the way home," Michael advised smugly.

Dizzy was renowned for her awful and stinky reaction to eggs in her diet. Everyone knew to give her a wide berth after the consumption of anything egg-related.

Meanwhile, Ashley knew that she was onto something but was doing her best to try and find another solution.

"What's on your mind, Ash?" Ryan asked with a knowing look.

She knew that he was already on the same page, but she tried to remain detached. "Oh, I'll keep you posted." she replied with a wink, followed by a long sigh.

"That brain is always working overtime, isn't it, Sis?" Michael teased.

She smiled and took a sip of champagne. "Yesit'll probably get me in trouble one of these days."

Michael grabbed another piece of chicken. "As long as it's your brain and not your food."

"Michael." She reached over and pulled his ear, making the men laugh good-naturedly.

"Aw, you know I'm joking. I never doubted your cream puffs, Sis. Don't give up; I'm sure you'll figure it out before too long."

"Thanks, brother of mine," she replied.

They went back to the water to pull their kayaks to their cars. Ashley took a moment to look around her at the glorious scenery of the marshland. There was the sandy shoreline abutted by tall seagrass marshes, the very Seagrass that gave the town its name. She saw a white egret standing tall in one of the marshes, perched as still as he could be and watching for fish he could snatch from the water. Just off the shore, they passed a big sea turtle swimming in the shallow water, his spotted head bobbing above the water as his four legs and shell were moving just below the surface.

The turtle. Ashley's blood froze, and she mentally backed away from the realization growing in her mind. She grabbed her phone and flipped through the photos she had taken in Eddie's trailer. When she came across the shot of the bedroom, she zoomed in on the bed-side table to the pile of women's jewelry. There was a pair of gold teardrop earrings and a sea turtle necklace. Hope's sea turtle necklace. The one that she was wearing the day before the picture was taken, that she claimed to only take off when she showered. Why, Ashley thought, would Hope go over to her estranged fiancé's trailer, much less leave the necklace there?

CHAPTER 15

RUNNING THE TIMELINE in her head, Ashley realized that Hope must have gone to Eddie's trailer the evening after their visit. That's why she had to excuse herself in such a hurry. She had needed to get to Eddie's right away, before Ashley did.

"Let's get the kayak back to the rental office before it closes," said Ryan. She was so lost in her thoughts that she didn't hear him. He finally waggled his fingers in front of her face.

"Earth to Ashley." He chuckled as his fingers danced and teased.

She laughed and slapped his hand away while she snapped back to attention. "It was Hope. I'm not sure why she did it, but Hope killed Colleen."

Ryan looked at her, astonished. "What?

How do you know?"

Ashley grabbed her phone and showed him the photo. "This necklace that was in Eddie's trailer the day we visited him belongs to Hope. I know that because I saw her wearing it less than a day earlier. She wouldn't have gone to his trailer if they were estranged, as Eddie told us, but she would go there to warn him that I overheard his fight with Colleen so they could create a cover story together."

She looked down at her hands and felt the tears welling. All her childhood memories of growing up with Hope were mixing in with the facts and clues, like a horrible kaleidoscope. It didn't seem possible that her old school friend could be such a callous, calculating murderer.

"The two surveys...Bobby only ordered one. The surveyor said himself that there was only one official survey but that two were conducted. I think we were wrong in assuming Eddie ordered that second survey; it was Hope. Why would Eddie try to convince Colleen to keep it a secret if he knew that she was going to die in a matter of hours? If he was planning to kill her, he would have already had the poison in hand, so their argument would have been pointless."

She paused to fish a tissue out of her purse and blew her nose as quietly as she could.

"I hate to say it, but it's obvious now that Hope did it. She must have known Bobby's deal with Bayview wasn't final yet, so she was trying to sell the land behind his back to the mining companies interested in the mineral rights for the property. While her father started to slip into the early stages of dementia, she took advantage of the lack of oversight and made some business deals without his approval. Oh, my God, it's so horrible. I can't believe it."

Ashley shook her head in disbelief, angry with herself for not seeing the clues sooner, even though she'd been led astray by all the other conflicting clues in the case.

"You know, this whole time I was imagining

how Emma or Eddie could have accessed the McCays' garden and the poison, but I totally overlooked Hope, who had easier access than anyone."

"She was the keynote speaker at the banquet, wasn't she?" Ryan asked. "She was talking in her speech about her dedication to preserving the ecological systems of Seagrass. What an outrageous lie."

Ashley blew her nose again, anger overcoming her feelings of remorse and finally streamlining her thoughts into a cohesive whole. The events of that night were rolling around her brain like thunder. Now she had all the pieces of the puzzle, and the light was finally breaking through, illuminating every dark corner and revealing the truth.

"How do you think she did it, got the poisoned puff to Colleen?" Ryan asked.

"You know, Colleen talked to me during the banquet planning. She requested that the dessert be served immediately after her speech, not before or during. I just assumed the request came to her from Bobby, but now I see that it was probably Hope. It gave her the opportunity to personally pass out the desserts at her table."

As they pulled into Bobby's bait and tackle store, Ashley knew that they had no option.

"You know, we have to go straight to the Sheriff. Can you call Mueller and ask him to meet us at Hope's house in 15 minutes? I'll go inside and pay for the kayaks while you do that," Ashley said.

Ashley started to make her way to say a quick thank you when Ryan stopped her and gave her a quick hug.

"Everything's going to work out, Ash. I'll call Mueller, and we'll finally get the justice that Colleen deserves."

Ashley smiled up into his open face, feeling her heart flutter for a moment.

"Thanks, Ryan. You're such a wonderful guy."

"Naturally." he quipped, before digging his phone out of his pocket.

Before she took off for the shop, she let Dizzy out. The dog promptly followed Ryan. She marveled at how Dizzy might as well have been Ryan's dog or, for that matter, Michael's dog too. It made her feel good to know that, if anything ever happened to her, Dizzy would have somewhere to go. Wondering why she would think such a thing, she shook her head and laughed at herself.

Once inside the bait and tackle store, she noticed Bobby wasn't at the desk, so she rang the service bell and waited for him to come from the back room. She admired the kayak paddles hanging in neat rows behind the desk.

"Hello, Ashley," said a woman's voice. She turned to see Hope looking at her and stopped in her tracks before walking slowly over to the cash register. She could feel her heart pounding in her chest, and when she realized that Hope wasn't smiling, she took a deep breath to steady herself.

"I thought I'd find you here." Hope's tone made Ashley's skin prickle.

"Oh?" Ashley forced out a tight smile, noticing how small her own voice sounded.

"Yes. My father tells me that you've been asking some interesting questions about our land, which I think is strange, but you've always been a snoop, haven't you, Ashley?"

She stood rooted to the spot, mentally kicking herself for not asking Ryan to come in with her. "Well, I..." She wasn't sure of the best approach. Did Hope know she knew? Probably. "Why did you do it, Hope? You have so much going for you here; I don't understand why you'd risk it all."

"You know, Ashley, I'm tired of everyone in this town assuming that I only earned my success based on what my father gave me, despite my many achievements in life. I'm sick of everyone thinking of me as the ditzy daughter of a powerful man. I'm done with the people of

Seagrass. What a bunch of back-stabbing, mean-spirited rubes you all turned out to be."

She stared at Ashley with such hatred and disgust, as if holding her personally responsible for her predicament. Ashley did her best to keep her cool while Hope continued to blather.

"I was planning to prove to you all that I can do it on my own, by selling the land and moving out of town to start anew."

Ashley glanced out of the window as Hope slowly walked towards her. Ryan was playing with Dizzy while talking on his phone; if only she could alert them somehow.

Hope was still talking. "You know, I'm smarter than most of the people in Seagrass put together. No one ever believed in me, and I'm tired of being underestimated."

Ashley once again found her mouth moving before her brain engaged, although she didn't have a single clue as to how she was going to get out of this one. "But, Hope, selling your father's land to get the seed money for a new start isn't exactly making it on your own."

Time seemed to stand still for a moment as the women stared at each other. Ashley could've kicked herself for blurting out that much, but she knew that it needed to be said. Without warning, Hope grabbed a paddle and lunged at her in a furious rage, eyes bulging and her face contorting, like a monstrous version of her former self.

"HOW DARE YOU!" she screamed, barely missing as Ashley ducked and darted to the left.

"Hope, please." Ashley pleaded as she tried to make her way to the door while scrambling and doing her best to avoid the swooping paddle. She felt it connect with her back as she darted away, panic overriding the realization that she'd been hit. She could feel the pain, but she reminded herself that it hadn't connected with her head. Still, she continued to duck out of the way as Hope continued her onslaught.

"Hope, stop it." she yelled as she tried to

make it to the door.

With an unholy screech, Hope lunged again, swinging the paddle violently over Ashley's head and missing her by only a small margin. Then the door burst open suddenly, and Ryan charged in, Dizzy close behind. Ashley dragged her out of the way as Ryan snatched the paddle and threw it over his shoulder, pinning Hope to the ground and yelling to Ashley.

"Sheriff Mueller is on his way, Ash. Go out and meet him."

"No, no, you don't understand. Get off me." Hope screamed.

Ryan was doing his best to keep Hope down. She was swiping at his face, but he managed to secure her arms to her side. Ashley went over to help. Slowly but surely, Hope gave up, crying in a hopeless heap on the floor while Ryan stood over her.

The police turned up only a few minutes later. Hope was hauled off to jail, again screaming like a banshee, while Mueller stayed behind to get the details.

"You know, darlin', I always had a feelin' about that girl."

Ashley and Ryan gave each other a look. Then he asked her if she was hurt.

"She only got me once. On the back, but I'm okay."

"Are you sure? Maybe you need to go to a doctor, just to make sure?"

She was touched by his concern, but she didn't want to be a cry-baby. "No, honestly, I'm fine."

Mueller seemed to be oblivious to this conversation. He had his thumbs hooked in the loops on his pants as he stared at the ceiling. "Ya just never know, though, do ya?" Shaking his head, he turned to leave. "It's over now, Ashley. Y'all go on home."

It took hours for Ashley to totally calm down. At a catered brunch the next day, she was able to tell her whole crew the story.

"I was the one who accidentally tipped off

Hope that Eddie had fought with Colleen. She went to Eddie right after I left her house, and they concocted a pretty convincing story about an affair between Eddie and Colleen. Poor Eddie, he actually had no idea about any of it. One of Gahn's employees—who had a conscience— emailed the information to Colleen. When she confronted Eddie, he tried to get her to keep it a secret long enough for him to talk to Hope about it. It must have been shocking for him to realize Hope was a killer, but his love for her— and her family's wealth—blinded him enough to go along with the lies."

"So how did you find out?" Sabine asked.

"We saw Monty Gahn at the estuary, which couldn't have been right because supposedly he was in Houston. It turns out that Bayview Corporation was just a shadow corporation that Hope and Monty Gahn set up in order to trick Bobby and Eddie into the deal."

After Ashley finished and all the chatter had died down, Mark raised his coffee cup in the air.

"A toast to the Dynamic Duo."

Sabine corrected him. "No, the Terrific Two-some."

Maude scoffed. "You're both wrong. To the Slimy Sleuths."

They could have heard a pin drop as everyone looked at each other. Maude meant well but she could be a little "off center." Patty broke the silence.

"Well, I'm just glad your head wasn't knocked off, partner. Although, I would've paid top dollar to see Hope losing it."

Maude laughed. "Wouldn't take much, hon. She's a mere slip of a girl, but not much room for the crazy."

Ashley agreed and slid a sidelong glance at Ryan, who winked and grinned back at her.

"Well, I just wanted you all to know our cream puffs are innocent, and I'm hoping that tomorrow will be business as usual."

"To innocent cream puffs." Ryan cheered,

making them all laugh and raise their coffee cups in unison while Dizzy barked her excitement.

Ashley finally felt the stress slowly slipping away, even though she was still coming to grips with what had transpired. True, she'd lost what she thought was a good friend, but when she looked around the room at the loving and supportive faces surrounding her, she felt her heart fill up with warmth. It was a hard lesson to learn. Nothing was ever set in concrete, no matter how much you butt your head against it.

CHAPTER 16

OVER THE NEXT two weeks, the town buzzed with the news about Hope and her hand in Colleen's death. People pulled up related plants and flower gardens, replacing them with agreeable flora and started campaigns to outlaw Brugmansia altogether. Of course, Sheriff Mueller was talking to anyone who would listen about the investigation. "We were on the trail of the killer, no doubt, but that Ashley Adams, I tell ya, she's got some snap in her garters."

He made it clear that without Ashley and Ryan's investigation, Hope would still be at-large and Colleen's death would still have been a mystery, not to mention the steady decline of Seagrass Sweets and The Southern Bird.

Now the opposite was true; Ashley and Patty could barely keep up with the flood of orders and bookings. The phone was ringing off the hook, and their internet orders had tripled. They even had to hire more staff to keep up with the demand. The icing on the cake—so to speak—was that Ashley's cream puffs were a huge hit once again. Everyone from gothic hipsters to showoff daredevils ordered them by the case.

Seagrass Sweets and The Southern Bird had also been subject to an onslaught of requests from all the newspapers and TV shows in the area. They'd even had many people calling from all over the country for an interview or sound bite. It was novel to start with but soon became tiring.

Ironically, a huge catering event was booked by a group most suspected to be the Localists themselves. Ashley and her business became the toast of the town, so the event was partially to thank her and celebrate her investigation. Summer was finally cooling off and autumn was creeping in, giving the local landscaping companies a reason to join the celebrations. They called the event "Fall into Food," which made Ashley cringe, but she went along with it for the sake of the business.

There was a sumptuous porcini mushroom risotto made with champagne and white truffles, along with flavorful pumpkin and almond soup, marinated cherry and chicken drumsticks and sweet onion tarts that made all who tasted them swoon. The biggest buzz was generated by the gorgeous desserts, which had nearly caused Ashley to go into a giant meltdown. She knew at the beginning that she was probably biting off more than she could chew, but she managed to come through with flying colors.

First, there was the blackberry and lavender panna cotta with French meringue and caramel, followed by deep-fried, cream cheese ice cream with raspberry sauce, and a pear custard and rum bundt cake. Patty scolded her for going way out of her league, but she was pleasantly surprised when Ashley rose to the occasion.

As the event opened, Ashley stood trying to keep from weeping tears of pure joy while the members of the community filtered past, stopping to congratulate her and give her a series of warm hugs and well-wishes. She'd followed Patty's lead and bought a sweet, crimson off-the-shoulder, summer dress, which made her look like she'd stepped out of a fine upmarket catalogue. The finishing touches were a lovely hairdo swept up from her shoulders along with delicate makeup.

When Ryan arrived, he snuck up behind her before she saw him.

"Ashley? Is that you?"

"I hope so." she replied, jumping a bit before turning around to face him.

A smile slowly grew across his face and he raised his eyebrows. "Look at you, all gussied up," he said, with an exaggerated Texan drawl.

"You scrub up nicely too." This was all she could come up with, as she was taken aback by his reaction.

They walked over to their table together. The setting was loaded with so many tea lights and hanging chandeliers that the fire chief worried about it being a disaster waiting to happen. Even so, the evening went without mishap, and everyone was enchanted with the fine food and classical music, which was provided by a small local chamber group.

Patty nearly fainted when Lee asked her to dance. In private quarters, she might be more likely to respond favorably, but being in front of the staff apparently made her nervous. It wasn't until Ashley kicked her under the table that she gave in and allowed him to lead her to the dance floor.

After their dance, she went and helped him clean up in the kitchen. He was shy when he thanked her for teaching him so much about cooking and the catering business.

"Well, I've learned a lot from you too, Lee—so—thank you too."

Ashley thought that their shyness was sweet, and she secretly hoped that one day they'd get together for real.

"What's on your mind?" Ryan asked, startling her out of her daze. She looked at him, wondering if it was just the wine going to her head or the mixture of soft lighting and lovely music. It all seemed like a dream.

"Can we go for a walk along the river?"

"Why, certainly, ma'am." he teased.

By the riverbank, she drummed up the courage to finally thank him for saving her life. "You know, I don't know what I would've done if you hadn't rescued me from Hope. Really. She could've killed me, and you risked your life for me."

"Well, I imagine you would've done the same for me."

She smiled and clasped her hands together in front of her as they continued to stroll.

"Yes, I would have, but you put yourself in danger. That means so much. I've never had a friend like you."

"I've never had a friend like you, Ash. I have fun when we're together."

She felt nervous, not knowing what to say or do. Spending time with Ryan usually came so easy. Now, under the orange glow of the Harvest Moon and in the aftermath of their successful sleuthing, she told herself she was getting all worked up for nothing. A little voice popped in her head. "You had your chance, it'll never work out now." She silenced it by thinking "one foot in front of the other." They walked a few more minutes in comfortable silence together.

"Ashley," said Ryan, stopping to face her. "I want more—more fun, more adventures, more you."

The moon was so bright that even here, far from the lights of the party, trees had shadows. Why was it that she always wanted what she couldn't have and then, as soon as she could, she wasn't sure that she wanted it any more?

"I've been so happy since you came back, Ash," continued Ryan. "That's not a coincidence."

"Thank you, Ryan, but I don't know." She paused. "What we have is so great. I'm afraid we'll mess that all up if we rush into something more."

Ryan took her hands into his. "Fine. We won't rush. How about this–let me take you to dinner."

Ashley looked first at their clasped hands and then into the eyes of her friend, which were filled with a confidence she couldn't resist.

"Dinner sounds great," she said, "as long as it's not at the Smokeground. That's much too messy eating for a date."

"Well, it's a date, then," Ryan said, squeezing her hands in his. They turned back to return to the party, hand-in-hand.

THE END

Letter from the Author

Thank you so much for reading. I hope you enjoyed this story and will consider writing a review on Amazon.com or lending it to a friend.

To be the first to know when the next book in the series and other new releases are out, join my email list online at

www.SandiScottBooks.com

I love to stay in touch with readers and periodically give out free books, advanced copies, and other fun stuff.

Stay cozy,
Sandi

Dear Readers,

Here's my gift to you--the first chapter of the next book in the Seagrass Sweets series – *Tarte Tatin Murder*. Find the entire book online at Amazon.com by searching for Sandi Scott or typing this short link into your browser:

getBook.at/tarte

TARTE TATIN

MURDER

SANDI SCOTT

A SEAGRASS SWEETS COZY MYSTERY

Tarte Tatin Preview
CHAPTER 1

"Merciful macaroons!" exclaimed Ashley, slamming on the brakes and barely missing the man in a CURE Cancer T-shirt and an absurd straw hat that covered his forehead down to his eyes. He waved vaguely in her direction as he zoomed away, the piles of sponsorship signs in his cart so high that he couldn't actually see her. Dust shrouded several people walking across the lot as the cart zipped past them, too fast and too close for the crowd.

Still grumbling about the cart driver's carelessness, she looked around the parking lot for more hazards. The other volunteers scurried about the lot, taking care of last-minute details for the non-profit cancer research foundation's golfing fundraiser. She had parked her van as close to the clubhouse as possible and jumped out to open the back just before she was almost mowed down by the reckless cart driver.

One of the volunteers waved and shouted, "Are you okay? That guy's a menace with all those signs piled on top of the ice chests and that stupid hat blocking his vision. And he didn't even stop to make sure you were all right; so rude!"

Ashley waved back. "Yeah, I'm fine; he just startled me. With this many people milling around in the parking lot, I can't believe he'd be that careless; some of them aren't moving nearly fast enough to get out of his way in time. It would be a pretty depressing start to the tournament for someone to be hurt before they even got inside the club. Anyway, it looks like a good turnout of helpers today."

The volunteer reached the back of Ashley's van. "For sure—it looks like we'll have plenty of people to cover things for once. And, speaking of covering, I'd better hustle my bustle. I'm supposed to be checking in the golfers starting in three minutes, and those old goats get testy if you make them wait. The sooner they get started, the sooner they can get back to the bar, and that's the only reason some of them play golf in the first place."

Chuckling, Ashley paused to admire the landscaping at the front of the club—red and orange double hibiscus, yellow esperanza and blue plumbago, and an iron picket fence with an arched gate twined with butterfly vine, its unique seed pods looking like butterflies hovering. Picking up a tray of scrumptious French pastries, she headed for the rather plain wood and cinder block building and tugged open the heavy, ornately carved door. Her eyes widened as she took in the opulence of the place—marble floors, gilded wall sconces, crystal chandeliers, heavy velvet drapes. "I don't think we're in Kansas anymore, Toto—or in little ol'

Seagrass, Texas, either! I don't know whether to be impressed or appalled!" As she turned in circles, lost in taking in the spectacle, she didn't notice any of the people wandering around her, their voices fading into a vague murmur.

She jumped as a deep voice said, "Welcome to the Seagrass Country Club!" Turning, she saw a young man, decked out in a formal business suit, standing at a small carved cherry wood desk just inside the door. "How may I assist you today?"

"My name is Ashley Adams; I'm the dessert caterer for the CURE fundraiser. Where should I set up the food?"

"If you will follow me, I'll escort you to the banquet room. The foundation is using that room during the day for light refreshments before the awards ceremony this evening. Do you need assistance unloading your desserts?"

Ashley wasn't about to turn down the offer. "That would be great. It's pretty warm out there today, so getting the chocolates inside as quickly as possible is probably a good idea!"

The young man pulled a small walkie-talkie from inside his jacket. "Hank, please come to the banquet room to assist the caterer." A short blast of static followed, and the young man continued, "Hank should be here in just a moment; if you'll excuse me, I'll get back to directing incoming traffic. Some of our members feel neglected if someone isn't there to call them by name as soon as they walk in the door."

Another young man stepped around the corner, this one in dress slacks and a short-sleeved shirt embroidered with the country club logo on the pocket. He grinned at her as he held his hand out to shake hers.

"Hi! I'm Hank. Greg said you needed some help carrying something?"

"Hank, thanks! I'm Ashley, and I have pastries and chocolates to bring in for the CURE fundraiser. I definitely appreciate your offer to help!"

"Oh, yum—that sounds good! We'd better

get them in quickly; we wouldn't want them to melt before the golfers get to taste them. They can sometimes be a bit fussy!"

As Hank and Ashley returned to the clubhouse with the next load, Hank commented, "I noticed you looking at all the glitz—pretty over the top, huh?" Clearly, he'd seen the same reaction before and found it amusing.

Ashley laughed. "I can't decide if it's beautifully sophisticated or if it's really cheesy and tasteless! It's hard to imagine that something this sumptuous is in little Seagrass! And you certainly don't expect anything like it when you see the outside. I know the merchants' association has been pretty successful in getting a more well-heeled type of tourist, but this has been here longer than that, hasn't it? And old Seagrass screams beach shack and barbecue joint. The décor here just doesn't fit that image."

"Some things don't change," Hank replied. "There have always been people with more money than common sense, and folks who saw the need to show off that money. The club has been around since the early 1920s, but it wasn't 'old money' that built it. The original members were definitely nouveau riche, and pretty snobbish about it! We read some of their journals and the newspaper accounts of the opening and events in my local history class. It was pretty obvious that cliques and arrogance aren't just a modern invention."

The last trays and boxes set on the table, Ashley thanked her helper and handed him a cream-filled mini profiterole. "Here, take a pastry with you."

The high-nineties temperature and 83 percent humidity had made carting in the miniature eclairs, stacks of hazelnut and chocolate crepes, and bite-sized *tarte tatin* squares hot work. Before she started arranging the pastries on silver serving trays, she stepped over to the bar, looking for a glass of water.

"Please tell me you are here with my liquor

order," the bartender, a petite blonde, begged. "As you can see, this bar is almost dry, and that won't do at all. The CURE guys are hoping for a big take on the fundraiser, and folks always bid higher at silent auctions when they're a bit lubricated beforehand."

"Sorry, I'm just the dessert caterer; I can't help you with the alcohol thing at all. I was hoping I could get a glass of water to cool off while I finish setting up. My name is Ashley; I own Seagrass Sweets, the catering company. "Geez, I'm sorry! The supplier said the delivery's on the way; it should have been here yesterday, but he said the order had never been placed. He thought he could get it here two hours ago, but I haven't seen any sign of the truck or the booze. I guess I'm freaking a little. Some of the members are already grousing about having to wait for their first drinks."

Ashley glanced at her watch. "Really? It's not even ten o'clock in the morning! Are they really looking for alcohol this early?"

"I guess some of them prefer hooch to hot coffee; we had to start locking up the stuff because a few of the members would help themselves to drinks before we open up at eight most mornings." She scooped ice into a large glass and filled it with water, then handed it to Ashley. "I'm Stacey. Just let me know if you need anything from the bar. It's going to be a long day for both of us!"

Carrying her drink back to the dessert table, Ashley covered the serving tables with the vintage tablecloths she'd inherited from her great-grandmother, which were with tone-on-tone flowers and vines embellishing the light ivory linen background. She used dainty pastel-stitched lady's handkerchiefs in place of a runner to add a subtle touch of color. With the antique tiered porcelain dishes and engraved silver trays, the table was elegant but still exuded warmth, a "high society meets country chic" effect that didn't take itself too seriously. The effect was subtle enough to accent the food without distracting from it, and Ashley felt a twinge of pride as she surveyed the display. She knew Great-Grandmother Estelle would approve of the way Ashley was using the heirlooms and that she would be proud of her great-granddaughter's business, especially because at least half of the recipes were from the handwritten cookbooks Ashley had inherited from her.

As she arranged eclairs, cream puffs, and slices of opera cake on the tiers and filled the crepes with chocolate-hazelnut spread and raspberries before dusting them with powdered sugar, an attractive silver-haired man wearing a CURE polo shirt and plaid golfing slacks walked up. His moss-green eyes twinkled, implying a friendly, charming personality with a hint of mischief lurking inside and giving Ashley the impression of a slightly naughty young boy hiding in a grown-up body. She wondered briefly what he'd been like as a child.

"Hello, there—you must be Ashley! I'm

Charles Brady, Ryan's uncle. After all the great things Ryan has told me about them, I can't wait to sample your desserts!"

Ashley smiled and offered him her hand. "I'm so glad to meet you, Mr. Brady. Ryan said that you would be here today. He used to mention you occasionally when we worked together at SmithCorp. He always told me that you were just like a father to him."

"Oh, I know you worked together; Ryan's told me a lot about you, and not just about your baking!" Ashley blushed a little, wondering what exactly Ryan had told his uncle; she had a hard time just trying to figure out what Ryan thought of her. "I have to say, though, his catering recommendation made one part of this crazy event simple for the planning committee." He winked at Ashley, making her blush even more. She knew that Ryan had been interested in her when they worked together, but she was involved at the time—with the wrong guy, as it turned out—a snake who led her into some illegal hacking while lying to her about both the IT work and their relationship. She wasn't sure that Ryan was interested now in anything more than a casual friendship. Maybe Uncle Charlie would drop a clue or two.

"It's a good thing I was a Boy Scout growing up," he said, tapping the etched silver flask tucked into his breast pocket and nodding toward the bar. "I came prepared for an emergency, and it looks like we have one over there—not a drop of Scotch whiskey in the place. What kind of bar has no alcohol on hand?" Based on the way he listed slightly to the side, Ashley suspected he'd already breached his emergency stash more than once that morning.

Before she could respond, a yelp from the silent auction tables startled them. They turned to see an older, distinguished-looking man pretending to brush non-existent crumbs off the front of a pretty young brunette's blouse.

He had her trapped between two tables, leaning close and leering, and her eyes were flitting around desperately, looking for an escape route.

"Ah, yes," Charlie remarked. "My golf partner for the day, the brilliant Oliver Green, genius researcher, and self-proclaimed gift to women, has already begun his play. He's closer to finding a cure for cancer than anyone else in the world, but he rather lacks the social skills necessary to charm women—or anyone else, for that matter."

As they watched, the couple's interactions became more and more awkward. The woman's body language said clearly that she wasn't interested in his advances but didn't know how to reject them without offense, and she kept trying to find a way to move away from him. Green, however, was totally unaware that she was repulsed rather than intrigued, and he kept sliding closer and closer, clearly ignoring polite society's usual personal boundaries.

"Excuse me, Ashley. I'd better go rescue our lovely volunteer before she either faints dead away or screams for her lawyer to sue us. It was a pleasure to finally meet you, and I look forward to getting to know you better." Charlie touched Ashley warmly on the shoulder as he walked over to Green, slapping him on the back and starting a conversation, giving the grateful volunteer a chance to escape.

Ashley pulled out her phone and quickly texted Ryan.

"*Thx tons for job referral. Just met ur uncle —great guy!*"

Her phone beeped seconds later.

"*Beware crazy Uncle Charlie. There's no telling what wild things he'll get up to!*"

For more information about author Sandi Scott and her cozy mysteries, please visit her website:

www.SandiScottBooks.com

NAPOLEAN-A CREAMY PUFF PASTRY CAKE

Ingredients

For the dough:

2 10"x10" (25cm x 25cm) puff pastry sheets

For the cream:

1 cup sugar

1 cup flour

1/4 gallon milk

3 large eggs

Preparation

1. First prepare the dough. Depending on the manufacturer of the puff pastry, you might need to defrost the dough, and either rollout or cut the sheets to the desired size.

2. Preheat the oven to 400F. Line 2 cookie sheets with parchment paper. Bake each puff pastry sheet for 20 minutes on the middle rack. After 10 minutes you might want to rotate the cookie

sheet 180 degrees to ensure equal baking. When the pastry is puffed and light
golden brown it is ready.

3. Let the puff pastry cool, and then cut
    each sheet horizontally into 2 layers,
    basically making 4 thin sheets. You will
    need 3 of them for the actual sheets
    and 1 for decorative crumbs, which you
    can easily make with your fingers.

4. Now for the cream: Beat the eggs with
    the sugar and flour. Boil the milk.
    While the milk is warming, pour about
    1/2 cup into the egg mix and stir well
    to gradually increase its temperature.
    This way the eggs won't curdle when
    you add them to boiling milk. Repeat
    this step 2-3 more times as the milk
    approaches boiling temperature.

5. Once the milk boils, pour the warm egg
    mix into the boiling milk, constantly
    stirring, to prevent lumps from forming.
    Keep on the stove for several 3 more

minutes, continue stirring. It's best to use hand held mixer in this stage.

6. Remove the cream from heat, let cool, and spread on the puff pastry sheets, creating alternating layers of puff pastry and cream (3 layers of each type, 6 total).

7. Spread the pastry puff crumbs on top of the upper cream layer.

8. Refrigerate for 2-3 hours or overnight before serving.

Makes 9 servings at 392 cal/serving

Recipe from Foodista.com

Made in the USA
San Bernardino, CA
09 August 2017